Yellow Rose of Texas

A Novel

DENNIS SNYDER

Concerning Life Publishing
Spring Lake, Michigan
www.Concerninglife.org

Cover image courtesy of koratmember / FreeDigitalPhotos.net

Acknowledgments

Thanks to my lovely wife, Vicki, for sacrificing her time to make this book a reality. Without her help this would be an impossible task.

A special thank you to the Word Weavers International Muskegon/ Grand Haven/Spring Lake writer's critique group for their encouragement and honest assessment of this work.

Chapter One

Standing with his hands resting in the small of his back and staring out the window at the streets of Austin, Governor Halford Abbot Bent was startled from his daydreaming by the pleasant and familiar voice on the intercom.

"Governor, Colonel Bowie is here."

Walking over to his desk, the Governor rested his finger on the button and responded, "Send him in, Delores."

"James, it's good to see you," he said shaking hands with the descendant of Jim Bowie.

James was a tall, handsome man, with coal-black hair and a stern yet endearing face. James Bowie was a pure Texan in his mid 50's. He loved his State almost as much as his beautiful wife Malinda. He was willing to die protecting the Republic of Texas. Even if it meant emptying his gun into any who would burst through the door just like the original Jim Bowie had done at the Alamo.

"Hello, Governor Bent, it's been awhile since we've talked. I'm pretty sure I know why you called, but I would like to hear it direct from your mouth. I don't want to assume anything of this magnitude."

"I appreciate that Colonel. Please have a seat. It looks like the last four years under President Obama is going to continue. It's hard to believe that the majority of the United States is willing to give up even more freedom. With the election of Watson for President, things are not going to get better."

"Governor, if I remember correctly, Lord Woodhouselee, has been quoted with the sequence of the world's greatest civilizations.

'From Bondage to Spiritual Faith
From Spiritual Faith to Great Courage
From Courage to Liberty
From Liberty to Abundance
From Abundance to Selfishness
From Selfishness to Complacency
From Complacency to Apathy
From Apathy to Dependency
From Dependency back into Bondage'

"So it stands to reason after two hundred and forty years as one of the greatest civilizations in the world that we come to this end. Our current

President took us from apathy to dependency and it is clear the President elect wants to control everything, bringing us back into bondage."

"You remember that from your days at the Naval Academy?"

"Yes sir, they gave me some great training and military strategies, that have served me well in the U.S. Marines."

"Colonel Bowie, here are the facts. Over 25 percent of Texans have already signed a secession petition. Of those surveyed, about 60 percent would also go for it. I have decided to do an all out effort to get a minimum of 51 percent to sign the petition to secede"

"Governor, I have to ask. Have you realistically thought this through? You're talking about a major change. Can we survive? Is it legal?"

"Before we get into the politics of it, and yes, we do have the right to do this, I've talked with Reverend Bob Wayne about the biblical mandate of seceding. I thought it would be wise to consult God's Word on things before we went too far."

"Pastor Wayne's a great guy. What'd he have to say?" Colonel Bowie asked.

"He quoted Romans 13 and said that the government, during the writing of the Epistle, was corrupt. That the administration of most of the Caesars was evil. Most were bi-sexual and threw lavish orgy parties. They heavily taxed their citizens, using that tax money for all kinds of idolatry and immorality. They became more and more anti-Christian and were heavily in debt."

"That sounds awful familiar, doesn't it?" James said shaking his head.

"The Reverend went on to say, neither Jesus or the Apostle Paul said to overthrow it but to follow it. However, the Bible does not tell us what to do when the government abrogates it's responsibility. When it does not fulfill the role of punishing those who do evil and instead punishes those who do good." Governor Bent stood and paced as he continued.

"I asked the Reverend about our founding fathers and the fact that they rebelled against the domination of British rule. He said that he believed that Britain became an illegitimate government authority."

"That's when I brought up the point in the Texas Constitution, both the 1836 original and the current, that states --- '*All political power is inherent in the people ... they have at all times the inalienable right to alter their government in such manner as they might think proper.*'

"We then talked about the lack of religious freedoms that we've experienced the past four years and the fact that many pastors can no longer preach the unadulterated Word of God. He said that he has been threatened with legal action if he continues to spew hate mongering from his pulpit.

"When I asked him what he meant by that, he told me he was simply preaching about sin and some called him judgmental and if he kept it up they would sue for defamation of character."

"Governor, did he give the go ahead or not?" James asked sitting forward in his chair.

"Colonel, he said that as far as he could see, we had an obligation to make sure that the Word of God could continue to be taught. We should fight for the freedom of all religion. He believes that the current regime has become anti-God. They make the bold statement that if anyone claims to have absolute truth, they must be silenced."

"Good, I would not want to be out of God's will in this kind of endeavor. Which brings me back to my first question. Is it legal and can we survive?"

"Not only is it legal, I believe, wholeheartedly, that we don't have a choice but to pull out. Joining the "Union" was always voluntary, which makes voluntary withdrawal an equally lawful and viable option. As far as, can we survive, without a doubt. We're very self-sufficient in our resources. We have our own energy grid and more oil and natural gas than we can use. The problem will be the far left in our State and perhaps Austin itself. This city is the most liberal in the State. They're going to claim that my administration is off-base with this."

Austin Texas, a bastion of liberal politics in an otherwise conservative State, was going to be the hard sell for the secession of Texas. It is the home to over ten institutions of higher learning including the University of Texas at Austin and was voted the number one college town with almost half of it's residents holding at least a bachelor degree. The City is also the home of many Fortune 500 high tech and pharmaceutical companies.

Many Californians had migrated to the surrounding area when their State went bankrupt in 2014. With the diverse make up of university employees, government workers, foreign and domestic college students, businessmen, musicians, high-tech workers and blue-collar workers Austin would be a hotbed of differing opinions. Fortunately for the Governor he had a conservative legislature in place.

"They can always move out of our country and move back to the United States of America. We've got a very strong State military and since they closed the federal bases down we have access to some great hardware that was left behind. My men will follow me wherever I lead them, the Texas militia can be mobilized within twenty-four hours. You know as well as I do, they all have a half dozen rifles and plenty of ammo. In fact most of them ignored President Obama's 2013 executive orders changing the gun laws. We've got thousands of semi automatic assault rifles and pistols."

"Well, Colonel Bowie, I would like to do this as peaceably as possible. All of us have friends and family not living in the Republic. Some would be put into detention camps as sympathizers and others might have to fight against us. I don't relish the idea of another civil war with brother against brother."

"I couldn't agree with you more Governor. So what is the next step?"

"I need you to become the head of our Department of Defense. That will make you the highest ranking officer over all of our military, State security forces, the Texas Rangers and you'll have final jurisdiction over all the State and local police agencies."

"Why me, Governor? You have higher ranking officers than me."

"James, the work you did along the Mexican border the last two years was remarkable. You helped set up the most elite force of border patrol agents in the world. You trained them to shut down the drug cartels that had infiltrated our State and you've kept them out. You're the man for this job."

"Thank you. But we were under State Martial law then and we could move and respond in like kind with those monsters."

"We never removed ourselves from martial law and I am expanding it to cover the entire State, or should I say, Republic, to protect our borders from tyranny and chaos."

"One of your first tasks will be to find qualified and like-minded leaders for all the agencies just like you did for the border patrol. Unfortunately, we need to get these men and women in place before anyone catches on to what we are up to. The news hounds can't figure this out until we are ready to announce our plan to secede."

"Governor, that's not going to be an overnight task. Talk is gonna happen. People are going to wonder why we're replacing some of our top officials."

"Yeah, I know. We'll spin some kind of talking points to confuse the press. I've got a lot of behind-the-scene stuff to line up before too much gets out. I'm quite positive that we'll be able to handle the situation. At least for awhile. I'm going public with a press conference 20 minutes after President Watson takes the oath on January 20th. That'll give you only 74 days. Lieutenant Governor Brody, two members of my cabinet and Delores are the only ones that know what's happening at the moment. I think that's about it James. You've got a lot to get done."

"For sure. I guess I better spend tonight with my wife and let her know that I'm gonna be a stranger for quite some time. Sir, I think you've made the correct decision. I'll check in as often as I can. Have a good day, Governor Bent."

"Thanks, James, but before you go, let's have a word of prayer together," he said as he reached out for Colonel Bowie's shoulder and bowed his head.

Chapter Two

"Sally, you need to see this," called Robert Lazier from the den.

"I'll be right there," his wife answered from the kitchen.

Robert and Sally Lazier, make their home in the Upcountry of South Carolina. Robert retired shortly after Barack Obama was elected for his second term, after 28 years with the United States Marines. The salt and pepper shading of his buzz cut, brown eyes and weathered face spoke of his long and hard life. Sergeant Major Lazier had worked himself up to the second highest rank of an enlisted man in the Marines. Through it all, he faced seven tours in Iraq and Afghanistan during the War on Terror, with the 3rd Battalion, 7th Marines, better known as the Cutting Edge. His military training came in handy as the police chief of Walhalla.

Shirley, a petite brunette had served well as a military wife. Her eyes lit up whenever she was in the vicinity of her husband of 25 years. She was able to sell her medical practice when Robert retired giving them a sizable retirement income. There were lonely times whenever he deployed and she was glad her practice took up so much of her time. She enjoyed their time together now that he was home most evenings. Walhalla was free from any major crimes. A burglary, here and there, with a few domestic disturbances and a drunk driver from time to time. All in all it was just a nice quiet town. Not much for the chief to do during the evenings.

Entering the den, Sally began rubbing the back of her husband's neck as she peered over his shoulder at the website. "Whatcha got, Honey?"

"It's only been a few hours since the election and there are thousands petitioning for secession from the Union. Here read the South Carolina petition on the We the People site."

Sally began reading out loud.

"We petition the Obama administration to: Peacefully grant the State of S.C. to withdraw from the United States of America and create its own NEW government.

As the founding fathers of the United States of America made clear in the Declaration of

Independence in 1776:

"When in the Course of human events, it becomes necessary for one people to dissolve the political bands which have connected them with another, and to assume among the powers of the earth, the separate and equal station to which the Laws of Nature and of Nature's God entitle them, a decent respect to the opinions of mankind requires that they should declare the causes which impel them to the separation."

"...Governments are instituted among Men, deriving their just powers from the consent of the governed, that whenever any Form of Government becomes destructive of these ends, it is the Right of the People to alter or abolish it, and institute new Government..."

"Are you thinking about signing this?" Sally asked alarmingly.

"Baby, I'm seriously giving it some thought and prayer. What do you think?"

"Robert, You know I'm in the same political camp you are. I think what our government has done over the past four years could easily warrant us signing to secede. My only concern would be the fall out from signing. I read somewhere that the president might take the citizenship away from those who sign a petition like this."

"I know we've given a lot of our freedom away and have, for all practical purposes, become a socialist country. But not even the President has the power to remove someone's birth citizenship. At least, I don't think we've gone that far. Although, it is hard to say what President Elect Watson will do when he gets into office next January.

"I think we should sign and voice our concern with the direction the liberal government is taking us. I've seen far to many young men give their lives protecting the freedom of this great country to sit by and not be heard."

"Okay sweets, let's sign. Go ahead and register us and fill in the forms. I've given my shoulder for a lot of wives who've lost their husbands fighting for our freedoms. I was always fearful I'd receive one of those visits from the chaplain. I was grateful when you decided to retire," she said leaning down and kissing the top of his head.

"Did you leave something on the stove?"

"My dinner!" Sally cried, as she ran into the kitchen. "Looks like you're taking me out tonight, Sergeant Major."

"Smells like it'll be better than eating that charred mess. Let me sign the petition and we'll run over to Captain Jack's Seafood Emporium for a

Lobster dinner."

"That sounds good. Maybe I should burn the food more often," she said dumping the freshly blackened roast in the trash.

"No way, baby. I'll take your cooking over any restaurant food," Robert said as he walked in and hugged her from behind.

"Don't start something you can't finish, mister. You're gonna have to woo me with lobster before any of that hanky panky stuff happens," she said with a smile slipping out of his arms.

"I'm holding you to that."

Chapter Three

Inauguration Day, Friday, January 20, 2017

"Delores, get me Colonel Bowie on the phone please."

"Yes sir, Governor Bent. Right away."

"Colonel Bowie, this is the day we've been waiting for. Do you have everything in place?"

"I believe we are all set, Governor. There are troops at all the major highways leading into Texas. We've taken over all the military bases that were shut down and I have people in place to take over and shut down the two federal bases still active. They both have skeleton crews compared to two years ago. We should be able to gain control without any problems."

"I have already been in touch with our people in Washington. They don't know for sure what's up yet but I've called them home. They should all be back into Texas before I announce.

"I'll be conferencing with the Governors of our surrounding states. I'll be asking them to stand behind us or at least to not interfere. I'm sure that New Mexico will be our biggest headache. Louisiana will most likely want to join us and Oklahoma and Arkansas will just try to avoid all of it and not take any sides.

"A half hour later the President will be sworn in and then I will make my announcement to the press. As soon as President Watson says the oath, you start the ball rolling and close off the new Republic of Texas."

"Governor, I have to admit I'm a little jittery. I served in the U.S. Marine Corp for 30 years fighting for our freedom and I regret that now I'll have to fight against her for the same freedom we've enjoyed all these years."

"Colonel, I too regret that it has gone this far. Unfortunately, I see no other choice. The current administration has raked us over the coals and the new one is gonna be twice as bad. Are you up to the task?"

"A little late to be asking that question now. But, yes I am and I, once again, pledge my support to the Republic of Texas. Governor, I will be praying for you as you begin the process."

"And I for you."

* * * * *

"Robert, the Vice President was just sworn in and it's almost noon. Better come now if you want to see President Watson's oath of office, " Sally Lazier called out.

"I was just doing some Facebook stuff. Where are they at?"

"Duh, on the steps of the Capital Building."

"I know that. I meant in regards to the ceremony, wise guy," he said as he walked into the room.

"The President is just coming to the stage. Chief Justice Roberts is waiting for him."

"Chief Justice Roberts, wasn't he nominated for the position by President George W.?"

"Yeah. I 'm surprised he's still got the position. It has to be hard for him to swear in Watson. They're polar opposites. It's about to happen," quipped Sally

"Are you prepared to take the oath, Mr. Watson?" Asked the Chief Justice.

"I am."

"Please repeat after me.

"I, Nicholas Samuel Watson, do solemnly swear,"

"I Nicholas Samuel Watson, do solemnly swear,"

"that I will faithfully execute the office of the President of the United Sates,"

"that I will faithfully execute the office of the President of the United Sates,"

"And will to the best of my ability,"

"And will to the best of my ability,"

"preserve, protect and defend the Constitution of the United States. So help me God."

"preserve, protect and defend the Constitution of the United States. As I understand it."

"Thank you Chief Justice Roberts," said President Watson as he held out his hand.

"Um. Congratulations, Mr. President," he responded with a questioning and confused look.

"Did you hear that," cried Sergeant Major Lazier jumping out of his chair. "He left God out and said, 'as I understand it.' That's not the proper oath!"

"Calm down honey. Let's hear what he has to say in his speech. Maybe he'll clear things up."

"He better. Shush, he's getting ready to

speak. Look at that pompous you know what. It makes me sick," he said as he paced the living room floor.

"Robert, sit down, you're making me nervous," Sally commanded.

"My fellow countrymen," he said holding his hands up in the air encouraging the crowd to quiet down. "Thank you for electing me as your 45th president. Former President Barack Obama, has done a great job in laying the ground work needed as we take this great country to the next level. He has been able to spread the wealth around and neutralize the power the wealthy have held for so long. We are all better off than we were eight years ago under the Bush administration."

"They still blame Bush for everything," Sally said.

"Shush, I want to hear this," Robert said indignantly.

"I want to address the words that I used as I was sworn in. I did not use 'so help me God', because I do not believe in a higher power of any sort. Like Teddy Roosevelt, I saw no need to use a Bible in the ceremony. As I read our Constitution, I understand it to say we are to keep God out of government. I will do just that. No more prayer in the Senate or Congressional sessions. No more government spending on Christmas decorations. In fact December 25th will no longer be a federal holiday. No more tax breaks for religious organizations. That alone will bring in millions, if not billions, to help with the 22 trillion national debt caused by the Bush tax cuts and the failure of the Republicans to follow our lead.

"I did not eliminate any of the official oath of office. However, I did add the words, 'As I understand it,' to the oath. I believe that we have been misinterpreting the intentions of our founding fathers for over 200 years. My team will be rewriting the Constitution and putting it in today's language. Once that process is done we will all be able to understand what it means.

"This is just the tip of the iceberg. I have so many plans and changes to put into effect, now that we have all three branches under Democratic control. I will be sharing some major things in the State of the Nation Address in a few weeks.

"One last thing, before the inauguration parties begin, I want to make sure you all know that I will not put up with any of this secession nonsense that has been hitting the Internet. I will not read or take into consideration any petitions that may be circulating. If you have signed one I would encourage you to remove your name by Monday morning or you will not like the consequences.

"Let the party begin."

"Wow! We are in for some tough times ahead," said Robert. "Our new President is going to take us to the bottom of World dominance. God is not going to be happy. I'm sure glad that He is still in control. I just wish I new what He had in mind letting this joker into office," he said pointing the remote and turning off the T.V.

"Honey, what should we do with our signatures on the seceding petition? Do you think he was serious about the 'or else'?" Sally asked reaching for his hand.

"I think we have no choice but to secede. I say we leave them on the list. What can he do? I'm gonna go see what the buzz is on Facebook and Twitter," he said walking out of the room.

Chapter Four

The tweets were flying about the inauguration speech as Robert jumped online.

Senator Hatfield tweeted, "I'm afraid of what our new President is going to do now that he has power."

The New York Times commented, "Finally we have a President who will do what needs to be done. Get God out of the picture."

The Blaze said, "The worst inauguration speech ever given. All hate and more bondage."

The battle was just beginning between the two sides when he received a Facebook notification from a marine buddy. Clicking onto his account he was not surprised at what he read.

"I am a Marine. I took an oath to protect my country against all enemies foreign and domestic. The way the United States of America is heading, forces me to invoke that oath. I am afraid I will have to stand up and fight against the country I love and my fellow Marines have died for. I cannot and will not allow the freedoms I have fought for be given away without a fight to the finish. I am not sure how to go about fighting this new administration. I'm looking for input on what to do. I am only a corporal and I need some direction. I know that I cannot be alone in my feelings. Please can one or two of my brothers in arms help me?"

"Robert, you need to see this," Sally cried. "There's a special news alert interrupting the inauguration parade."

"What's it about?" He asked as he entered the room.

"I don't know. Listen up. It's the Governor of Texas."

"My fellow Texans, and citizens of the United States of America, it is with heavy heart and a sound mind that I make this announcement. Please realize that we do not want anything but a peaceable resolution. As of 12:10 P.M. today, Friday, January 20th, 2017, the great State of Texas has seceded from the United States of America. We have become our own sovereign nation. Henceforth, we shall be called The Republic of Texas and I will take over the duties of President. Our Minister of

Defense, Colonel James Bowie, is at this very moment making sure that our borders are secure. All military bases located in Texas that were previously closed by the U.S.A. have been turned over to our control. The two remaining bases, Fort Hood and Goodfellow Air Force Base, will be allowed to stay open as long as the administration understands that they are located on international land.

"Our military strength rivals that of the United States in its diminished capacity. We are capable and ready to defend the Republic with our lives. Colonel Bowie is very capable of leading this great new Nation of Texas in any and all military action.

"Once again, I, we, desire a peaceable resolution to this secession. I am open to negotiations with President Watson on how to handle our break up amicably.

"If you are a Texas citizen, not currently living in Texas, I encourage you to make your way home as soon as you can. I know there are questions flowing through your minds at the moment. Let me assure you we can and must take this action to assure the freedom of the citizens of the Republic of Texas.

"Thank you and may God bless us, as we

step out in faith for our freedom."

"Sally, I am afraid, the battle has begun."

"What are we gonna do? Do you think other States will follow Texas? Will the Marines call you back to active duty?"

"Wow, slow down dear. One question at a time. I think the other States will see what happens with the Republic of Texas. For all practical purposes, Texas is the only State that could possibly pull this off and survive. What we're gonna do is take one day at a time and see what develops. Even if the Marines do recall me, I won't go. I can't fight for a country that refuses to believe in God. Actually, you better figure out what you can do without. If push comes to shove we're moving to Texas."

"I knew you would say that, as soon as I heard Colonel Bowie was the new Minister of Defense. How many deployments was he your Battalion Commander?"

"Five out of seven. He knows how to win battles and I'd fight alongside of him in a heartbeat. You know he's the one who led me to trust Jesus Christ as my Lord and Savior. I think I'm gonna head over to the bank and withdraw our savings. Give me a kiss. I'll be back in about twenty minutes."

* * * * *

9:00 A.M. Monday, January 23, 2017,
Police Chief Robert Lazier, arrived at his office.
While reviewing his schedule set for the new week
Mayor Bill Elliot stuck his head in the doorway.

"Robert, we need to talk."

"Morning Mayor, come on in. Have a seat.
Would you like a cup of coffee?"

"No thanks. I have some bad news for you. I
received a call today from Homeland Security."

"What'd those yahoos want?"

"They wanted to let me know that your
citizenship has been revoked."

"What," said Robert as he jumped out of his
chair. "They can't do that!"

"Apparently they can and they did. I have to
let you go immediately. Robert, you are fired.
Please clean out your desk and vacate the premises.
Leave your badge on the desk along with your city
issued weapon and ammo. Deputy Fife will take
over as acting Police Chief until we can find a
qualified replacement."

"This is hard to swallow. I served my
country for 28 years and this is what I get."

"I'm afraid there's more bad news. Your military retirement has also been revoked. Here's the paper work they faxed to me this morning," he said handing Chief Lazier the papers. "They also expect you to pay back the $192,000 they've already paid you for retirement. And, by the way, your bank accounts have all been frozen. You have five days to even things out."

"Like, that's gonna happen. What's our country come to?"

"Robert, You have until Friday at 4:00 P.M. to pay back the government or I have to arrest you."

Standing with his knuckles on the desk Sergeant Major Robert Lazier looked Mayor Elliot in the eye and said, "You and whose army! Here, take your badge and crap. This Marine is outta here," he said throwing the stuff across the desk.

"Bob, that's a city car, you'll have to walk home."

"You can pick it up at my house. No way I'm walking," Lazier said walking toward the door.

"Come on Chief, I'll give ya a ride," Officer Phil Davis said.

Phillip Davis, the newest member of the Walhalla Police Force, had only been back home for two months. He walked with a slight limp caused by the bullet still lodged in his left leg.

While on patrol in Syria, the former Army Private First Class, got caught in an ambush set up by members of the former ruling party. The Ba'ath Party, had been deposed April 2013, when President Obama sent American troops in to quell the civil war. Fighting continued through 2013 and the troops were called home in January 2014. PFC Davis was discharged in 2016 when the final military cuts were made.

"Thanks Phil. I appreciate the lift."

"Chief, I think it is a shame that you're being treated this way. Man, a decorated hero and all. How many times you been wounded fighting for the freedom of this country?" Davis asked as they drove away.

"Way more than I want to remember, son," he said rubbing the scar on his right side.

Chapter Five

"Governor Bent, excuse me, I mean Mr. President, We've got some issues at all the major roadblocks."

"Yes, Colonel, it's also been hard for me to get used to the idea of being a president. What's the problem."

"We are letting all those with Texas issued ID's through the check points but there are thousands of others who want to cross the border for asylum. I'm not sure we should let them all in? I need your input."

"I think we need to limit it to our own citizens until we know how President Watson's gonna respond. Turn everyone else away. Get their names and contact information, along with the date and time they requested asylum. When things have calmed down we will have a record of who wanted in and when."

"Will do, Mr. President. I'm sure we're gonna have a lot of immigrants crossing the border in more desolate areas. But we can deal with those folks later. We will let them know that if they give us their names now and we find them in Texas before they are invited they'll never get in. That might quell the unprotected border rush.

"There are a lot of smaller protests going on in all the larger populated areas. I'm heading down to Austin where the largest gathering has erupted. There are more liberals in the Capital than any other area of the Republic. I'll stop by your office when I get into town."

"That'll be good, Colonel, it's getting a little noisy outside. The crowd is growing. I just had a meeting with the majority of the Fortune 500 company CEO's. Most have agreed to stay out of the picture and try to keep business as usual. However, they would not control the free time of their employees. I imagine many of the protestors are high tech or pharmaceutical employees along with a university student or two."

"Yeah, that's my thought as well. Probably a few former Californians who left after they raised their taxes. I hope that left handed professional golfer isn't one of them," Bowie said with a smile.

"I'm sure there's very little military experience in the crowd so we should be able to quiet them down with little or no problem. Keep the faith, Mr. President."

"You too, Colonel. See you in the morning."

* * * * *

"President Bent, President Watson is on line one," buzzed Delores.

"Thanks, I'll take it and get Vice President Brody in my office ASAP."

"Yes sir, Mr President."

"Hello, President Watson. How can I help you this morning?"

"Governor, you can stop this nonsense any time. You are barking up the wrong tree if you think I'm gonna let you secede," he said irritated.

"Excuse me President Watson. Please address me with the same respect I give your office. I am President of the Republic of Texas and you will address me as such."

"That's a bunch of bull and you know it, Governor. It ain't gonna happen. You cannot secede from my country."

"Well President Watson, I didn't know it

was 'your' country. I guess we have nothing to discuss then. We have seceded and if you can't respect my office I have nothing further to discuss with you. Goodbye."

"That son of a – hung up on me," Watson said slamming down the phone. "Secretary of Defense Bennett, get your military ready. We are going to war! Texas is too big for it's britches and needs to be taken down a peg or two. I'll show him who's boss."

"Mr. President," interrupted Vice President Angelica Chandler. "You don't have the authority to go to war unless we've been attacked."

Angelica Chandler was an attractive 62 year old, graying brunette. She was the first female Vice President and was liberal as they come. Her partner of twenty years, Susan Giles, had encouraged her to run. She was a dark horse and an unlikely pick by the macho Watson. She was, however, the main reason he had won.

"They surrounded two of our military bases and refuse to let anyone off the base. That's an act of war as far as I'm concerned. I'm invoking Martial Law immediately. Get a press release out right away," he said to his press secretary. "Bennett get mobilized. We're not letting Texas get out from under us. They'll remain a State of the Union or be blown off the face of the map."

"Isn't that a little harsh?" Chandler asked with surprise. "We did campaign for an end to all wars worldwide."

"I want world peace just like everyone else does. But I'm in control now and Halford Abbot Bent is not gonna get away with this garbage. Not on my watch!"

"If that's the way you want to go Mr. President, we need to get to the War Room downstairs," Bennett said .

The War Room was actually the President's Emergency Operations Center (PEOC), located under the East wing of the White House. It can withstand everything except a direct hit from an atomic bomb. Since nuclear warfare was outlawed in 2015 by the United Nations, nothing would be able to touch the President as he proclaimed war against the Republic of Texas.

* * * * *

"Mr. President, Vice President Brody is here to see you," she said.

"Please send him in, Delores."

"Hello Adam."

"Hi Halford. I filled in the Legislature and

the majority are on board. Obviously some of the more liberal members were up in arms," he said shaking his head. "A lot of political bickering going on. The Senate approved by a two to one margin and the House agreed by a landslide. I was surprised so many of the Democrats are on board."

"That doesn't shock me. Even the Democrats don't like what Watson has in store for the USA. If it wasn't for the folks looking for a handout he would've never won."

" Yeah, once they found out they could vote themselves entitlements from the government it was all over," Brody said with a sigh.

"President Watson just called. He told me to call the whole thing off."

"I can guess how that went over."

"He refused to recognize us as free sovereign country and demanded loyalty. He tried to bully me into submission. I basically hung up on him. I'm assuming he is setting things in motion as we speak. Be ready for some swift reprisals."

"Colonel Bowie's got the borders secure, doesn't he?"

"Yes he does, for the most part. But the heavy stuff hasn't begun yet. Adam, your job is to keep the legislature in check."

"Yes sir. Will do," he said leaving the room.

Chapter Six

"What do you think is going to happen to us?" Sally questioned as she rested her head upon Robert's chest. Sally relished the comfort she felt when she was able to hold her man. He had an exceptional body for a 50 year old. A large chest, muscular arms and an abdominal muscle structure she would die for. She always felt safe in his strong arms.

"Honey, I wish I could read the future. The one thing I do know for sure is that God Almighty is in control. We can rest in Him as our refuge and strength. He is the all-powerful One. We can be safe in His everlasting arms."

"Thank you, Robert, for always pointing me back to Him. It's very comforting to me to know you trust our Heavenly Father for everything," she said leaning over him and reaching for the box of tissue on the night stand.

"Are you crying, Babe?"

"Yeah, I wish I had your sense of strength under fire. I'm just not made that way. I'm scared," she said blowing her nose.

"There's nothing wrong with being scared. I have my fears with this whole thing too. I just lost my job, my retirement's been revoked and my own men are going to have to try to arrest me on Friday if I don't pay up. And you know I'm not gonna do that."

"I still have my savings from when I sold the practice. We can live off that for a long time."

"Yeah, you better check that in the morning. We might want to get it out in cash before they freeze it like they did our bank accounts."

"I'll call them first thing in the morning."

"We better get some sleep. It's gonna be a long couple of days. We'll make some plans in the morning," said Robert as he threw his arms around his lovely wife and gave her a romantic kiss.

"Hey, I thought you wanted to go to sleep?" She asked pretending to fend his off.

"I do – in a little bit. Come here."

* * * * *

"Who in the world rings a doorbell at six in

39

the morning?" Robert thought out loud as he pushed himself away from his bowl of oatmeal. Positioning his 9mm pistol into the back of his waistband he glanced out the side window and saw a young couple nervously waiting.

"What can I do for you folks?"

"Are you Police Chief Lazier?" The young lady asked. Her husband glancing around the neighborhood for anyone watching them.

"I was until yesterday. If you need police help, you'll have to go down to the station."

"We just came from there. Can we come in? We're afraid to be seen by the wrong people," she said nervously.

Pausing for a second, as he summed up the possible threat standing in front of him and said, "Come on in. What is it you're afraid of?" He asked opening the door and standing back so they could walk in.

"Our US citizenship was taken away from us because we signed a petition to secede from the Union. We didn't think it was legal so we went to the police station to see what they knew."

"Really, and what did they tell you?" He asked as if he didn't know.

"Officer Davis told us to see you and gave us your address. Do you know what going on? Our bank account was frozen and they would be taking away our driver licenses if things don't change."

"Oh boy, its started. Come on into the kitchen and we'll get some coffee and chat about what I think is happening. I'm Robert Lazier as you know – and you are?"

"I'm sorry. Josh Daniels and this is my wife Addison," he said shaking hands.

"Everybody just calls me Addi," she said with a meek voice.

"Addi it is then. Have a seat. Do either of you take cream and sugar?"

"Who was that at the door? Oh, I didn't know we had company," Sally said quickly pulling her robe over her night clothes and ruffling her hair into some kind of order.

"Hey, good morning sleepy head. Good thing you didn't come out naked," Robert laughed. "I wondered how long you'd sleep in. This is Josh and Addi Daniels. They're looking for answers why their citizenship was taken away."

Sitting at her table was a handsome young man in his late twenties. His worn out, holey blue jeans, shaggy long brown hair, and horseshoe style earring in his left ear shouted independent attitude. His blond, long haired, lovely wife was obviously afraid to let go of his hand.

"When's your due date, Addi?"

"How did you know I was pregnant? I'm not really showing yet," she asked rubbing her belly with her free hand.

"A mother can tell. You have that glow about you that only belongs to those special enough to hold life inside of them."

"I'm only two months along. I don't know what we're gonna do," she said almost in tears. "Josh lost his job yesterday because he was classified as an illegal alien. We won't be able to stay in our apartment with no income. We were hoping your husband would have some hope for us."

"Addi, Josh," said Robert setting coffee in front of all three, "I don't know what to tell you just yet. I was let go yesterday for the same reason. My accounts have also been frozen. Sally and I were going to make out some plans today. You're welcome to join us. The more heads we can wrap around this the better. It wouldn't hurt us to have a younger perspective on the subject. Either one of you good with a computer?"

"Josh is a wizard on them," Addi said with an admiration only a wife could have. "He's an IT expert."

"Well, I can hold my own. Addi tends to

build me up," he said brushing the hair out of her eyes. "But they did pay me because of what I can do with a PC."

"Great you just might come in handy. Honey, why don't you whip up some breakfast for these two.? I'm gonna see if I can get through to Colonel Bowie."

"You know Colonel Bowie from Texas," exclaimed Josh. "I heard his name mentioned by Governor Bent yesterday. Are you planning on going to Texas? We want to go with you!"

"Whoa, hold your horses. We haven't laid out a plan yet. I was his Sergeant Major when we were both active duty Marines. He's a great military leader but I gotta talk with him before I head out West."

"Honey, that's your phone now. It's in the bedroom."

As Robert ran out of the room to grab his cell phone, Sally continued. "We have bacon and eggs, hot oatmeal or cold cereal. Which would you like?"

"That was our neighbor, Joe Clinton. He's gonna come over in about an hour. The same thing has happened to him," said Robert walking back into the kitchen. "There's gonna be a lot of people looking for answers about their citizenship. Our politicians are gonna be busy."

Chapter Seven

Colonel Bowie and his small contingent of Texas Rangers, led by Lieutenant Rudy Tucker, arrived at the Capital building at 9:00 A.M. to assess the situation. Tucker, an ex army special forces specialist, appeared to be very capable of handling the situation at hand.

"Lieutenant, I don't think you need me to take care of these protesters. What's the Ranger motto, 'One riot, one Ranger.' right?"

"Yeah that's it Colonel."

"Well you've got 65 men counting you and there's only a couple thousand of them. I'm gonna head up and see President Bent. You and I have already discussed what needs to be done with the antagonists leading this group. Try not to bust too many skulls but let them know we will not tolerate rioting on the streets of Texas."

"Yes sir," he said with a salute as Bowie walked away. "Ranger Wade, take 16 men and get on the other side of the Capital steps. Let people know that you are there and flaunt the fact that you're Rangers. Ranger Walker, take your 16 and spread out behind the main group. Williams, you take 12 and head right into the middle of the crowd. Use a little force as you make your way in but try not to antagonize them. Just enough to let them know you are in their midst.

"The rest of us are heading up to the platform. Make sure you spread out so they see Texas Rangers everywhere. We're gonna arrest everyone on the platform and any one else who looks to be a leader. Head out men,let's do it."

As the Rangers spread out amongst the protestors the crowd began to quiet down. Their reputation over the last one hundred and ninety years preceded them. The Texas Rangers were one outfit you did not mess with. Lieutenant Tucker and his men began to handcuff every leader on the makeshift platform in an orderly fashion. Moving to the microphone he said, "Listen up, I'm Lieutenant Rudy Tucker, with the Texas Rangers. The secession of Texas has happened, no amount of protesting will change it. The majority of our citizens desire this move. I am asking you all to go home. Go back to work. If you are a Texas citizen you are part of the new Republic of Texas with all the rights afforded to such. If you are not a citizen you have two choices and only two. One, you can get a green card at your local police station and eventually become a citizen. Two, you are free to leave our country in a peaceable manner. I repeat, these are your only options."

"What about those you are arresting?" yelled someone from the crowd.

"They will be processed and all Texas citizens will be released with a warning. Those who are not citizens will be deported as illegal aliens. I will not ask you again. Please disperse peaceably and do it now!" Tucker said as he waved his hand and pointed with his finger.

* * * * *

"Looks like your men have everything under control, Colonel," President Bent said watching the crowd disperse.

"I had no doubt they could handle it, Mr. President. They are the elite, when it comes to law enforcement."

"Without a doubt Colonel, without a doubt."

"Mr. President, Mr. Vice President, let me

show you on the map what we can expect from the U.S. Forces," Bowie said walking over to the map of Texas hanging on the wall.

"New Mexico is going to be the hot spot. I believe that the U.S. Marines from 29 Palms are going to move into the Northeast corner and bivouac around U.S. 40. They will spread out South perhaps as far as Clovis as they await their orders," he said pointing and moving his finger up and down the West border.

"That's my old unit. I know most of the officers and Colonel Shields and I were at the Naval academy together. He's smart and well seasoned. He'll be a tough opponent. His problem will be keeping his men unified. A lot of the Marines don't like the way the country has gone. Some may decide to defect. We'll have to be careful of spies infiltrating as defectors."

"What about the White Sands Missile base?" V.P. Brody asked. "Do we need to worry about missiles coming at us?"

"Probably not. They lost a lot of their funding under Obama. All they have left are long range missiles. I'm not an Air Force guy but I don't think they can get them redesigned to hit us. We're too close. I'll have to check that with our air guys to make sure. The may have some short range rockets but I'm sure we can handle them.

"All of New Mexico's bases are Air Force and for all practical purposes they have been shut down for the past couple of years. I'm going to concentrate the mass of our troops up in the Northwest corner. Our Air Force will be patrolling the entire border, including the Rio Grande, just in case Watson decides to make peace with the Mexicans."

"Our planes are older U.S. Planes, aren't they?" President Bent asked.

"Yes sir, Mr. President, but they are still state of the art machines."

"How we gonna tell them apart from the Union's planes? Aren't they all marked the same?"

"We've painted a huge yellow rose on the tail section and have replaced U.S.A. with the block letters, R.T. They're real easy to spot and any military aircraft that violates our airspace will be warned to leave immediately or risk being shot down."

"Thank you Colonel Bowie. Continue to keep me informed. If something should happen to me, V.P. Brody is totally up to speed to take over as President."

"Yes sir. I 'm going to leave Lieutenant Tucker and his men here with you. He and his men are very capable and will do their best to make sure nothing does happen to you."

"You think they would try to harm me? Bent asked. "I think that's pushing the envelope even for Watson."

"You can't put your guard down for an instance when it comes to war, sir. Now, if you will pardon me, I need to get to Amarillo."

"By all means, Colonel."

Walking out of the door Colonel Bowie's phone rang. "Hello Sergeant Major, how have you been?"

"I've been better sir. I just had my citizenship revoked and got canned. Apparently, I'm now an illegal alien. Looking for a country."

"Well, if you can get to Texas I have a spot for you in my command. I could use an experienced leader and combat veteran. A lot of my men are good ole boys that can kill a rat at 100 yards but have absolutely no military training."

"We're gonna try to make our way there but we are limited with how and when we can travel. The current administration is already setting up detention camps for those who signed petitions to secede."

"You said we, so I assume Sally is coming with you?"

"Of course she is. I also have a young couple in the same boat with us. He won't be much of a fighter and his wife is pregnant. But he does know computers like I know my M16 so he'll be a huge help for us as we travel. I'm assuming we'll pick up a straggler here and there as well. Hey, for all I know I might have an army before I get to Texas."

"Okay, Sergeant Major. I'll let all the roadblocks know you're coming. Have some sort of ID to prove to them who your are. And get here quickly. I've got a feeling things are gonna get bad."

"Will do Colonel. Keep looking up sir."

"You too, Robert, and be careful."

Chapter Eight

The 3rd Battalion, 7th Marines began to roll into the Northeast of New Mexico between Clovis and U.S. 40 led by Colonel Ryan Shields. Six hundred of the best fighting men the world has ever known were getting into position to invade the new Republic of Texas. The Texas militia, under Colonel Bowie's command, started to mumble amongst themselves as they watched the opposing forces set up camp. His rag tag team of seven hundred and forty-nine men were divided into 15 strategically placed units along the border.

Colonel Shields approached the road block with five Marines at his side. "I would like to speak with your commanding officer," he said in a confident voice of victory.

"That would be me, Colonel," Bowie said as he walked out from behind an armored vehicle.

"James, I didn't expect to see you on the front lines."

"Ryan, looks like we're in for an interesting time. It's been a while. How's the wife and kids?"

"They're doing well. How about Malinda?"

"She's a little nervous now that I'm back in action. I think she would rather have me retired and home."

"Why don't you stop this nonsense and go home then. You took an oath to protect and defend the United States of America. This amounts to treason."

"Ryan, I took an oath that said I would protect the Constitution of the U.S.A. from foreign and domestic enemies. I'm on the right side of this battle and you know it. The Republic of Texas will become a sovereign nation under God and I will fight to the very end if need be. I don't want to fight against my brothers of the 3/7. I know more of you guys than I do my militia."

"We have no desire to fight you either. But you'll give us no choice if you don't back off this secession stuff."

"Ryan, walk with me for a bit," Bowie motioned for his men to stay as they walked away. "How you been doing with your problem. You still got it under control."

"Don't worry about my drinking. It won't keep me from victory," he said looking James in the eye.

"I guess that means you're still at it. Man, I thought you had quit," James said placing his hand on Ryan shoulder.

"Don't preach at me," he said pushing the hand away.

"Okay," he said holding his hands up and backing away. "I'm just concerned buddy."

"I'm sorry, James, you've been a good friend over the years but I have my orders. You have seventy-two hours to stand down or we will be coming in."

"Colonel Shields," Bowie said walking back to his men. "a lot can happen in seventy-two hours. Be careful, many of your men agree with what we're doing. Sergeant Klink, how long you been the Sergeant Major?" He asked as he walked away.

"Sir, shortly after Sergeant Major Lazier resigned," he shouted back.

"I'm your commander now, Sergeant Major," Colonel Shields said in a gruff voice.

"Yes Sir, Colonel Shields."

* * * * *

Once back to the command building, Colonel Bowie summoned Captains Lewis and Cormac along with the fifteen lieutenants. Jack Lewis had spent twelve years in the U.S. Army ending his career as a Captain. He resigned his commission and moved back to his home State of Texas, six years earlier, to take over the family cattle ranch, when his father died. His hearts desire was a life in the military yet was grateful he got out when he did. He had seen the handwriting on the wall during his deployments and knew he would not be in agreement in the direction the Army was going.

Captain Dakota Cormac, an ROTC graduate of Texas A&M, served 6 years in the Army. The last year in Syria as a First Lieutenant. Neither were Marines but both had combat experience and could handle the men under them. Lewis commanded the 8 Northern divisions and Cormac the lower 7 divisions. The fifteen lieutenants answered to them.

"Men," began Colonel Bowie. "We've been given seventy-two hours to stand down or be invaded. We are not going to back off," Bowie said with the authority of a man who knew. "As you know, the engineering company spent the last two weeks setting up the front line. There's a watch tower every one hundred and fifty yards apart ranging from the Northern border down to Clovis. There's a trench running just about the entire length and it's been concealed and I doubt if the Marines know it is there. Every fifty yards is an escape trench about fifty feet long. You all should have had the opportunity to inspect them and know what's expected of your men," aiming his laser pointer to the large map on the wall he highlighted the trenches. "Five minutes before the attack you will position your men in the trenches. Make sure they're not spotted entering and do not give themselves away.

"Here in each of the towers," again pointing with the laser, "you will have two men stationed gathering any information they can from the enemy forces. Ten minutes before zero hour these two men will position dummies in their place. Don't make it obvious that they're dummies."

"Colonel," asked one of the young lieutenants. "Why take them out of the towers? Wouldn't they be able to help as spotters?'

"Good question, Lieutenant. The men we're fighting are the best trained infantry in the world. The first thing they'll do, probably simultaneously, is blow up each one of those towers. When they topple expect a ground rush. That is when you will be ready to take out any charging Marines. They will be sending some mortars and other artillery into the back bunkers. We'll catch them totally by surprise. Unfortunately, they will lose a significant number of young men. They will have to retreat to lick their wounds. Any more questions?

"No? The most important aspect of this, being a victory for us, is keeping the trenches a secret. I can guarantee they are watching us. You men be careful and do what you can to bring our boys home again.

"One of the reasons we are seceding is because the U.S. has taken our freedom of religion away from us. I'm going to pray for wisdom and protection. If you don't want to pray that's fine, we have freedom of religion in the Republic of Texas. However, you will have to stay in this room until I'm done. If you would like, bow with me.

"Our Gracious Heavenly Father, it is with a heavy heart that I have to give orders to kill young men and women as they attack us. It is not our desire to see anyone lose their lives. Yet, at the same time, we do not want to see our freedom taken away from us.

"Father, if there is anything you can do to stop this senseless fighting, please do so. We know you are all-powerful and that you are in complete control of every situation. We ask for your wisdom and guidance as we seek Your will above all else.

"Father, protect us as we fight for the Republic of Texas and the freedom of it's citizens.

"In the name of Jesus we ask these things. Amen.

"Okay men, do what's necessary. If you have the opportunity, take prisoners don't kill. Be careful, smart and alert. Dismissed."

"Hello Colonel Shields, I appreciate that you're still taking my calls."

"Hi James, what can I do for you?"

"You know, as well as I do, that we are going to fight and defend Texas. I am asking you to consider moving all your Texas Marines behind the lines. We don't want to see any deaths but it would be unconscionable to have fathers shooting at their own boys or brother shooting brother. We did that in the 1800's and I would just as soon not do it here."

"I agree with you James. I've already heard some rumbling about it in my ranks. I will do my best to keep them in the back. You be careful that you don't shot those who defect. I don't think there will be many but a lot of our boys didn't like the way Obama led as Commander in Chief. And we both know Watson will be worse. Don't quote me on that – I'll deny it. You have until Friday at 1:00

PM to surrender."

"That ain't gonna happen. You do realize that we outnumber you."

"Come on Bowie, you know that it'll take five of your guys to one of mine. Your untrained Militia doesn't have a chance. We're better armed and better trained. In fact you oversaw a lot of the training yourself."

"I think the British said the same thing right before we kicked their butts during the Revolution."

"Touche, James. Goodbye."

Chapter Nine

"Hello this is Robert Lazier. How can I help you?"

"Hi Chief, it's Phil Davis. I wanted to give you a heads up," he said nervously looking over his shoulder.

"Hey Phil, Call me Robert. I'm no longer gainfully employed by our fair city. A heads up about what.?"

"I overheard, acting Police Chief Fife, talking to some homeland security guy a few minutes ago. Something about allowing those who have had their citizenship revoked to get a green card. I guess there will be a news alert on all the major networks at 1:00 this afternoon. Thought you would like to know."

"Thanks Phil, I'll make sure we watch it."

"Hey Robert, just so ya know I'm behind

you all the way. I think that you all are getting the shaft. If there's anything I can do to help, this number is my personal cell."

"I appreciate that. If I ever need information, I may give you a call. Thanks again."

"That was Phil Davis one of my former officers. There's a special on the news in about twenty minutes. He thinks we'll want to watch it."

"I'll set my phone timer so we don't miss it," said Josh. "We'll probably be knee deep in thought as we figure out what we're gonna do. Addi," he said touching her arm. "Get a pen and paper and be our secretary as we talk things through."

Sitting around the Lazier kitchen table were Josh and Addi Daniels, Robert and Sally Lazier and their single neighbor Joseph Clinton. Joe, the oldest of the five, was 68 years old and an Army veteran. He still had the occasional nightmare of stalking through the jungles of Vietnam, constantly wet with rotting feet. He could still see the faces of his brothers in arms as they lay in their own blood.

"Ya know, fifty-eight thousand Americans were killed in Vietnam because we were afraid that communism would take over the world. It's been over forty years and the way things are going our country will be communist under Watson's rule," he said with a disgust ladled throughout his voice.

"He's already taking complete control now that Martial Law is in effect. I think we need to get to Texas and help them out."

"I'll have to agree with you, Joe. I talked with Colonel Bowie this morning and he said that they have a place for us if we can get to Texas."

"You know him?" Joe asked with surprise.

"Sure do. I was his Sergeant Major before we both retired. We worked close together and fought side by side in Afghanistan. He's a great leader. Okay, let's figure out our plans."

For the next fifteen minutes they discussed when they would leave for Texas. How they would go about it and the tasks that needed to be done before they hit the road. Before they knew it Josh's timer went off.

"We better turn on the news. The special alert will be on in two minutes," he said dismissing his phone.

"Here it is. Everyone be quiet," said Sally turning the sound up.

The President's press secretary started the newscast. "Ladies and gentlemen of the press corp. The forty-fifth President of the United States of America, Nicholas Watson."

The mostly liberal press stood and applauded the newly sworn in President Watson.

"Members of the press, citizens of America and to those who have decided to withdraw their citizenship by signing petitions to secede, I have a very important message to you all," he said as the clapping subsided.

"We will not be bullied. We will not allow States like Texas to secede from the Union. On Tuesday, January 24 at 1:00 P.M. we gave the State of Texas seventy-two hours to withdraw their request for secession. At exactly 1:00 P.M. Friday, January 27, 2017, should they not withdraw their demand, we will invade and forcibly take control of the State of Texas. I would encourage anyone living in Texas, who don't want to secede, to either change the Governor's mind or to move out of the State. The United States of America will not be responsible for collateral damage if you stay behind.

"As for those who have had their citizenship revoked. You can still survive in our country if you will register for a green card. The sign up process will be the same as it was two years ago when we registered illegal aliens. Once your forms are filled out, you will receive a tracking chip in the back of your hand. This chip will allow you to work and reside in peace. You also have until 1:00 P.M. January 27th to get registered. Anyone who does not register, and is caught, will be sent to a detention camp. Resist at your own peril. If you are stopped during the next seventy-two hours you will be asked to register on the spot. If you refuse you will be sent immediately off to a detention camp.

"As you know, Martial Law has been instituted and my orders will be carried out. Make no mistake about it, even though President Obama's administration cut back our military budget and troops, we have a strong enough force to topple Texas in one swell swoop. The particulars of the new immigration laws can be found at your local police station or posted at the U.S. Post Office.

"We are the United States of America and we will stay united even if it means wiping out the new Republic of Texas. That's all I have for you today. I'm sorry, no questions, I'm too busy to answer them, we're at war."

"There you have it folks. If you or a member of your family had their citizenship revoked get down and get registered before it's too late," the newscaster said. "Our President knows what he is talking about. No States can leave the Union. It is not feasible and it will do more harm than good. Please, all of us here at the newly formed Government News Broadcasting Company encourage you to get registered."

"Can you believe that, GNB! The President

created his own broadcasting company. Pretty soon they'll control em all." Sally exclaimed.

"Well gang, it looks like we have until Friday noon to get to Texas. Addi, let me see that list," Robert said, reaching out for it. "Joe, you've spent a few nights camping in the mountains. Figure out what we need to stay warm and survive the wilderness. We're gonna have to travel quietly and through isolated territory."

"No sweat. I think I have most of what we need in my garage," he said heading out the door.

"Josh, you're our tech guy. Use your credit card and buy us whatever electronic stuff you think we'll need. Make sure you get a dozen or so cheap disposable cell phones that can't be traced."

"Okay, I think a couple of laptops and i-Pads will work out for us. If I'm putting these on my cards, how am I gonna pay for them without a job?"

"Well, Josh. You're gonna be in Texas when that bill comes. Actually, I hope you're able to use your card. Here use this cash for the phones not your credit card so they can't trace them back to you. The cash I got out of my account on Friday won't get us very far so try to use the card for the other stuff."

"You know what, keep the cash, I'm gonna charge it to my former employer's card," he said with a smile. "That'll give em something to think about in a couple of weeks when they get the invoice."

"Sally, you and Addi head over to the grocery store and get whatever food staples you need. They should be non-perishable as much as possible. We'll try to pick off a rabbit or squirrel for meat as we move along. Here's some cash but try to use our card if you can. And Doctor Lazier, you might want to get any medical supplies you think we'll need."

"Okay, we'll put together a shopping list and medical bag. What are you gonna do?"

"We're gonna need some weapons. I've got my guns and some ammo but I think we're gonna need more before we get to Texas. I'm heading over to the gun shop to see what I can pick up. I think Slim, the owner, is sympathetic. He'll probably let me buy some ammo and a couple of crossbows. Be careful out there. I don't want you to get stopped and arrested."

"Give me a kiss and don't be so anxious you big worry wort. I took care of myself when you were deployed. Addi and I will be just fine."

Chapter Ten

The Cowboy Gun Shop was run by Chester "Slim" Miles who was as redneck as they come. His appearance reminded Robert of a rough and tumble mountain man. Slim was, however, one of the shrewdest businessmen he had ever met and one top gunsmith.

"Hey Slim. What do ya know?"

"If what I hear is true let me shake yer hand. Chief, did they really fire you?"

"I'm afraid so. Didn't like my politics I guess."

"Didn't like yer politics! Watson doesn't like anybody's if they doesn't agree with him. What can I do ya fir?"

"Come on Slim you're not fooling me. I know you've got an MBA so stop the redneck talk," Robert said with a smirk.

"Okay, but don't tell any of the good ole boys. They're my best customers and they think I'm one of them," he said rubbing his whiskers.

"No problem buddy. I need some ammo for my M-16 along with some 12 gauge shells."

"How many ya want?"

"All you've got. I also need some 38 specials and 9mm ammo for my pistols."

"I suppose you want all I've got in those too?" asked Slim with a cock of the head and a concerned look in his eyes.

"Slim, I've got some things to do and I'd appreciate our silence."

"I won't do any talking out of school. I'm pretty sure I know what you're up to. I've got a nice – don't tell anybody – but I've got a nice little AK-47 with no registration needed. Plenty of ammo comes with it if you want it?"

"I always knew you had some stuff you didn't want the Police Chief to know about. I'll take it along with two of your best crossbows and plenty of shafts."

"Take a look out the window," Slim said motioning with his head. "They pulled up as soon as you were in the door."

"Man, I'm being followed. My own officers turning on me. What's life coming to now-a-days?"

"Listen when you gonna need this stuff?"

"The sooner the better."

"Okay I'll drop it off at Joe Clinton's on my way home. That way no one will be suspicious. I think Joe's in our camp. It'll be there about 5:00."

"Hey man, I really appreciate this. Joe knows what's going on so it's safe to drop it off at his place. Put it on this card if they'll let you," he said handing over the VISA card.

"No sweat, but I'm calling the AK a compound bow. Since they've been outlawed it doesn't look good on the credit card receipt," Slim said with a wink of the eye.

* * * * *

"Can I help you sir?" Asked the clerk at Walmart.

"Yes you can. I would like one of those Asus tablets and the smaller Nexus one next to it. While you're in the case, I also need twelve of those prepaid trac phones."

"Twelve! I don't think we have that many? Let's see – I've only got nine phones, sorry."

"No sweat, I'll take those and a couple of car chargers for the phones and the tablets."

"While you're getting those things together

I've got to go pick up some other things. Can I pay for everything back here?"

"Yes sir, that'll be no problem."

Josh headed off to the front of the store where he had seen some flower bouquets. Picking up a cute group of Chamomile he turned and started to walk away. Pausing in the isle, he turned back to the flowers and put the cheaper flowers back and grabbed the most expensive bouquet of roses.

"Here, put these roses on the bill," he said handing the clerk his credit card.

"Yes sir," she said looking at the card. "This is from A-1 Computer Applications. Do you work there?"

"Yes I do. Part of the IT team. That's why I'm buying all these techie things. Here's my ID card," he said slipping her the card.

"Thanks, but why the flowers?" she asked cocking her head.

"They've got me out here buying this crap on my own time. I figured they could spring for some flowers for my wife."

"You're so sweet. I wish my husband thought of me like that," she mused ringing up the items. "Here you are sir. Have a great day and I hope your wife enjoys the flowers."

"She will."

* * * * *

"Addi, you start getting the stuff on our list and I'll head over to the pharmacy area and put together a medical bag."

"Okay Sally, come find me when you're done."

Sally grabbed a cart and pushed off to put together a first aid kit. Ibuprofen, bandages and gauze, a half dozen tubes of antibiotic ointment, two tubes of hydro cortisone ointment, one gross latex gloves, a box of alcohol wipes and a breathing barrier for mouth to mouth. Thinking out loud she said, "With what I have in my old medical bag this should do it."

"What was that you said, Sally?" The store pharmacist asked.

"Oh, hi Bill. I was talking to myself. I didn't see you."

"Yeah it was pretty obvious you were caught up in your own little world,"he said with a snicker. "Looks like you're putting together a first aid kit. You know we sell them all ready put together."

"I know but this is a special one."

"I'm so sorry about Robert's job. I heard he was let go. What happened?"

"Just a little misunderstanding between him and the mayor. We'll be fine. I appreciate your concern. I think I have all I need."

"You want to pay for that stuff here or the front counter?" He asked motioning with his hand toward the counter.

"I'm here with a friend so I'll just go find her and pay up front. Thanks Bill, we'll see you later."

"Sally, I'm over here," called Addi.

"Have you found everything we need? I'd like to get out of here before I meet up with someone else to explain things too."

"Yeah, I think I have all that was on the list. Let's check out. You want to use your card or mine."

"Let's try mine first."

"I'm sorry Mrs. Lazier. Your card has been denied. Your credit limit has been used up."

"Just the credit limit used and not closed completely?" She asked.

"Looks like some high priced items were just purchased putting you to the limit," he said pointing to the screen.

"Here try mine."

"Yes ma'am," said the cashier as she swiped

the card. "That one worked. Sign in the box, please.

Chapter Eleven

The Lazier two-car garage was beginning to look like an apocalyptic survival store. Joe had his camping supplies laid out on the right hand floor: one large six man tent, a couple of two man pup tents along with three back packs and two gas lanterns with white gas fuel and an extra bag of wicks sitting alongside a gas camping stove complete with what looked like a 50 year old Boy Scout folding set of pans and eating utensils.

The girls had the camp folding table set up with all the powdered milk, flat breads and a small water purifier in case they ran out of bottled water. The medical supplies were already placed into two smaller bags alongside Sally's medical bag. The electronic stuff Josh had picked up was still in the boxes, except for the Asus tablet that he was busily setting up for the trip.

On top of his work bench, Robert was loading extra magazines for the M-16 and AK-47. His 38 Special and Clock 9mm were fully loaded and both 12 gauge shotguns stood up against the wall.

"Joe, you were in Vietnam, do you know how to use this M-16?" Robert asked.

"I don't tell a lot of people this but I was Special Forces and have been trained on just about every weapon out there. I've got 24 known kills but then that was in the late 60's I'm a bit older now and I don't relish adding anymore to my list."

"I'm with you Joe but we may not have a choice. It'll probably come down to us or them. If we can keep to the mountains and back country roads all the way to Texas we might get lucky.

"I'm thinking that if we head into Tennessee then down to North Georgia and Alabama skipping across the border between Tennessee and Alabama into Mississippi near Corinth, then southwest into Louisiana near Nacthez and then down to Beaumont Texas."

"Sounds like you got a route. I would suggest we take two vehicles just in case. I've got a couple of old walkie-talkies that are so outdated no one would be able to trace. But they still work within a couple of miles. We should take your minivan and all I've got is a pick-up."

"I've got a Jeep," said Josh overhearing the conversation. "It's four wheel drive just in case we gotta go off road. I've even got a gas can strapped to the back."

"Great. My minivan and your Jeep it is. Sally, why don't you and Addi take the vehicles and get them gassed up. Make sure the can on the Jeep is full and fill these two five gallon cans up. We'll take tomorrow to load everything up get all the last minute stuff handled and head out early Thursday morning."

"Okay," said Sally as she reached up for a kiss. Robert stopped what he was doing and gave her a big hug with the kiss. "Did you see the nice bunch of roses Addi got from her man?" She asked with a cock of her head.

"Yeah. What's the deal Josh, trying to make me look bad!"

"I don't think that'll ever happen. I've seen you two lovebirds in action. You can't keep your eyes or hands off each other."

"She's the love of my life. Outside of the Lord, she is the most important person in my life. Okay ladies, get out of here," he said giving Sally a slap on the rear as she walked away.

"You've mentioned God a number of times.

One of these days you'll have to tell me why He's so important to you."

"Well Josh, I would imagine we'll have some extra time during our upcoming adventure. I don't suppose you know how to use a gun?"

"I've never shot a real one. Used to have a BB gun when I was a kid but it never really interested me much. But I have played a lot of military video games."

"I can show you how to use one but we can't fire it here. Too noisy. Why don't all three of us head down to the basement and set up a target range for the crossbows. I can teach you how to shoot them. They may come in handy when we don't want to make any loud noise."

* * * * *

"Mayor, are you sure you want to do this? Police Chief Lazier was liked by an awful lot of town folks. You might be biting the hand that elected you," said Interim Police Chief Bernard Fife.

"You have your orders. At first light on Thursday you and your men arrest Lazier and his wife as illegal aliens. They gave up their right to be U.S. citizens when they signed that petition. I want

77

to make sure we set a precedent for anyone else who might have secession in their minds," he said scowling. "If they refuse to get a chip in their hand send them off to the detention camp up in Illinois. That will encourage anyone else who chose to leave their country to get a green card and chip. The Laziers can be our example and we get them outta our town."

"Okay, but you know there might be gun play involved. We followed him to the gun shop Tuesday. Didn't look like he left with anything but I personally know he has a couple of pistols and an M-16."

"Well wear your Kevlar armor and take them by surprise If you've got to take them down go for it. They're enemies of the country and we need to deal with them."

The Mayor walked out of the Chief's office as Fife reached for his phone. "Hello Phil, I need you here by 6:00 in the morning. We've got a serious bust so bring your swat gear. Give officers Bennett and Casper a call and make sure they're here at the same time."

"Okay Chief, who we taking down?"

"I'll tell you all in the morning. Get to bed early it's gonna be a tough collar."

* * * * *

With both vehicles packed, parked in the garage and ready to go, Robert went over the plans one last time with everybody.

"Okay, any questions? No, then let's get some sleep we're hitting the road at 7:00 tomorrow morning. Set your alarm clocks for five and we'll eat a good breakfast and finish getting ready."

"Honey, I'm scared," said Sally leaning her head on Robert's chest.

"I know, Baby. It's sort of like the first deployment over in Iraq. I didn't know what to expect as a PFC, so I was anxious. After the first couple deployments and I knew what was going down I was better. Still anxious, but better. I'm not sure what to expect as we deploy to Texas. I think the trip there's gonna be hard no telling who or what we'll run into."

"Robert, I don't pretend to understand what God's doing but I do know the two I trust the most in life are leading me, God and you. I will follow wherever you lead."

"Thanks for the confidence. I just hope I'm making the correct decisions. It's not just the two of us anymore. Hey, we need to get some sleep, morning will be here before ya know it," he said leaning over to give her a kiss.

"Not so fast big boy. This might be the last chance we'll have alone for quite some time. I'm leaving you with something you'll remember," she said pushing him onto his back.

"Oh, you little devil," he said with a big grin.

Chapter Twelve

The next morning, Police Chief Fife, Phil Davis and officers Bennett and Casper met at 6:00 AM to discuss the bust.

"We're all here Chief, who we going after?" Phil asked.

"You all got your swat gear? This is gonna be dangerous. I can almost guarantee a firefight."

"Come on Chief, this is Walhalla we don't have anyone that tough around," Officer Bennett said with a sneer.

"We have orders to arrest Robert and Sally Lazier."

"Whoa, what did they do? I thought they had until Friday?" Phil said.

"The Mayor wants to make an example out of them. Apparently we have thirty to forty other folks who have lost their citizenship. The Laziers

81

either have to take the chip or be deported to a detention camp in Illinois. The Mayor figures if the toughest guy in the county is busted, everyone else will see the futility in fighting the system and they'll come on their own free will to get registered as aliens.

"Here's what I figure we'll do. Davis, you and me will take the front door. Bennett and Casper the rear. At exactly 8:00 I'll call Lazier and tell him they're surrounded and to come out hands raised to avoid any gunfire. I'm hoping that he'll want to protect his wife and they'll come out peaceably.

"However, he's been around the block when it comes to warfare so stay behind cover. He's a crack shot and is feeling a little let down by his country."

" A little let down! Come on Chief, they ripped everything out from under him. He spent his whole life protecting our freedom and we do this to him. We ought to be honoring him not arresting him," he said angrily.

"Phil, I'm just following orders and I expect the same from you. Understood!"

"I'll do my job, I just don't like it."

"Okay then finish getting ready. We leave at seven. If you've got any religion it would be good to say a prayer or two," said the Chief as he walked into his office.

"Hey guys, I'm gonna go out and have a smoke, be back in a few," said Phil pulling his cigarettes out of his pocket.

"No sweat, you got about an hour before we gotta leave," said Casper.

* * * * *

"Let's go people. It's 6:00 time to get outta bed and ready for breakfast. We need to be outta here by eight if we want to make any time today," yelled Robert in his best Sergeant Major voice.

"Man, you sure can bellow," grumbled Josh. "You'd think we were in the Marines."

"Get used to it, I run a tight ship," he said with a grin.

"Honey, can you get the phone? I just cracked an egg," said Sally.

"Hello."

"Robert?"

"Yes."

"Phil Davis, listen I haven't got much time but you gotta get outta town now. In less than an hour we're coming to arrest you and Sally."

"On what charges?"

"Being an illegal alien. We're coming in

83

swat gear so unless you want to be arrested or get into a fire fight you need to get going. We're leaving the station at seven," he whispered nervously looking over his shoulder.

"Thanks Phil, I owe ya big time."

"Just get going. I'll try to stall but you need to get. I gotta go."

"Okay everyone, we've got thirty minutes to hit the road. The police are coming to arrest us. We need to be outta here before seven. Hustle people. Let's get movin. Forget about breakfast and grab your stuff."

"It's starting isn't it?" Sally asked.

"I'm afraid so Baby," he said as he grabbed his wife and gave her a big hug. Looking her in the eyes he continued, "It's gonna start getting dangerous for all of us. Looks like we're gonna begin our travels with a price on our heads. Trust me Baby, Lord willing, we'll make it to Texas," giving her a peck on her forehead he yelled, "Let's move people. Grab a piece of toast as you do your stuff. It'll be a while before we eat again. Butter a few more pieces, Babe, I'll get all our stuff together."

Josh, Addi, Joe and Robert walked through the kitchen a dozen times as they grabbed their belongings and loaded them in the vehicles. They each grabbed a piece of toast or cup of coffee each time. Sally was busy putting together some sandwiches and packing up the last of the food to take with them.

"Come on get in and check the walkie-talkies," yelled Robert. "Testing, testing, do you hear me Josh."

"Ten-four, hear you loud and clear."

"I'm opening the garage door. Josh, let me back out first and come out right behind me. We're heading northwest into the mountains. Over."

"We're right behind you." said Addi. "I'll be manning the radio while Josh drives. Believe me, he needs both hands on the wheel. I've seen him drive," she said with a chuckle.

The minivan and Jeep pulled away from the quiet neighborhood and out of sight at the same moment the entire Walhalla police force pulled up in front of the Lazier residence.

"Looks like they're still asleep," commented Chief Fife.

"I don't guess they have anywhere to go," Officer Davis said. "He lost his job and she retired last year. They're most likely sleeping in. That'll give us some time to get into place as we wait for eight."

"I think we'll go in early. No sense putting it

off."

"Let's give everyone time to get set. I'm in no hurry to get shot at."

"Okay," The Chief said grabbing the radio. "Men. Get yourselves into position I'm making the phone call in fifteen minutes. Set your watches, it's now 7:15 at exactly 7:30 I'm ordering them out."

Bennett and Casper got into position, behind the shed, at the rear of the house. Chief Fife and Phil positioned themselves behind their cruiser as they waited.

"Hey Bennett, I don't relish getting shot at by Lazier."

"Me neither, Casper. I don't like the idea of shooting them either. They've both been good to us. But what can we do? He brought this on himself. Why'd he have to go and sign that petition to secede. I thought he was smarter than that."

"Maybe he is and we're the dumb ones. The good ole U.S. of A. isn't what it used to be. We sure have seen our freedoms disappear over the last four or five years."

"I know, but it's still our country and we need to do our jobs. Man I hate this waiting."

Chapter Thirteen

At exactly 7:30 A.M. Police Chief Bernard Fife dialed the number to Robert Lazier's home phone. He let the phone ring ten times before he hung up.

"What's the deal Chief?" Phil asked.

"No answer. They're either still in bed or waiting for us to try something. Bennett, you guys see any movement in the house?"

"Not a thing Chief," said Bennett pushing the button on his shoulder radio. "What do ya want us to do?"

"Sit tight till I figure things out. Phil, what do you think we should do?"

"Man, I'm not sure, you're the boss. Maybe you could go knock on the door," he said with a grin.

"And get my head blown off! No way that's

gonna happen. Pop the trunk and get me the bull horn. I'll call him out."

Officer Davis opened the trunk and rifled through the metal case pulling out the electronic bull horn.

"Here ya go Chief."

"Robert Lazier, this is Police Chief Fife, throw out your weapons and come out with your hands up. Don't make us come in there. Innocent people might get hurt."

The neighborhood sprang to a life of its own as people began to gather behind the police cruisers.

"What's going on officer?" asked a neighbor.

"You better find some cover. We're trying to arrest the Laziers," Phil said.

"They're not home. I saw them drive away about thirty minutes ago."

"What did you say?" Chief Fife asked standing up.

"The Lazier's minivan and a black Jeep pulled out of their garage about thirty minutes ago. Headed up toward the mountains. They're probably in Tennessee by now."

"Great. Bennett, you and Casper go in through the back door and check inside."

"You gotta be kidding. We're not going in

there and getting shot."

"The neighbor said they left thirty minutes ago. I think it's probably safe but don't take any chances be ready just in case."

The two officers approached the door, one on each side. Casper checked the handle and the door swung open. Bennett entered with his weapon at the ready swiftly scanning the room. "Clear."

Casper came in and they each went through opposite doorways, Bennett into the garage and Casper to the living room. They continued to sweep the house making sure each room was clear before proceeding to the next.

Bennett motioned toward the basement door. "Swing the door open," he whispered.

As Casper pushed the door open, Officer Bennett turned and dropped to his knees as he aimed his weapon down the stairs. He slowly stood and made his way down the steps until he reached the floor below.

Scanning the basement he reached for his shoulder radio and said, "All clear Chief. You can come in now."

"Chief, it looks like they cleared out in a hurry this morning," said Casper. "There's still some toast on the counter and the coffee pot is still on. I'd say someone tipped them off."

"The only ones that knew about it was us four," said Phil. "Either of you make a call?"

"No way," said Bennett. "We're faithful to the team. Didn't the Mayor know?"

"Yeah, but he gave the orders. I doubt he would've warned them."

"Maybe they were planning on leaving all along. It just happened to be at the same time we wanted them. Coincidences do occur," Casper said.

"I guess we'll never know. If they left our jurisdiction good riddance. I didn't relish a face to face anyway. Phil, get an all points bulletin out for them. Armed and dangerous."

"Okay, I'll head back to the office and handle that. You guys all set here?"

"Yeah, the three of us can sift through what's left. You go man the station," Chief Fife said.

* * * * *

Once back at the station, Phil settled behind his desk as he decided what to do next. *Oh man, do I put that APB out or not? If I wait too long the Chief will know I tipped them off. If I don't do it and he finds out I'm dead meat. What am I supposed to do? Come on Phil think!"*

"Susan, we need to put out an APB on Robert and Sally Lazier, driving a minivan with South Carolina plates number WL-63812 heading southeast. Get this to all law enforcement departments between here and the East Coast."

"Yes sir," said Susan the station secretary.

That should buy them a little bit more time. Phil was pleased with his deception.

* * * * *

"Hey Addi, can you hear me?" Sally asked.

"Loud and clear we're about a half mile behind you. Every so often we see your rear end on a straight away."

"Good," Robert said. "We're gonna stay on Warwoman Road until we get to Clayton. Then we'll stay on 76 till the 197 fork and take that down to Sautee. We'll stop there for gas and something to eat."

"Does Robert think they'll have a bolo out for us?"

"Come back with that. What's a bolo?"

"Sorry Sally, you probably don't watch a lot of TV. A bolo stands for 'be on the look out'. It's sort of like an all points bulletin."

"Yeah, most likely they'll be looking for us. We're gonna just keep driving unless we run into trouble or nasty weather. Ya never know about the mountains in January. Hopefully we don't hit any snow blocked roads."

"Okay, roger and out."

"Addi, I think you just say Roger," chuckled Sally.

"I've never used any of these old timer thing-a-ma-jigs. They're pretty cool."

Chapter Fourteen

"Colonel Bowie, you wanted up at six," said Lieutenant Stephens, knocking on the door.

Stephens, a lieutenant in the Texas Rangers, was assigned to Bowie's security outfit. His job, along with four other Rangers, was to protect the Colonel from those who might desire to assassinate him.

"Thank you lieutenant. I'm awake."

The Texas Militia's camp was set up just east of the Welcome To Texas sign located one mile from the New Mexico border. A small 10 room motel, situated on the U.S. 40 service road in Glenrio, served as the command post. Making up the compound, surrounding the motel, were rows and rows of small trailers and tents. A large pole barn, formerly used as storage for the road commission, was transformed into a mess hall.

"Attention," called out the young soldier nearest the door as the Colonel came into the mess hall.

"At ease men, finish your breakfast," said Bowie as he walked through greeting his men with a pat on a shoulder and nod of the head. "Good morning Private, I'll have some of those eggs, scrambled and a couple links of sausage please."

"Yes sir, coming right up."

Finishing his coffee the Colonel turned to Stephens. "Lieutenant, I need to head down to the Mexican border this morning. Make sure the plane is ready to go."

"Yes sir. What's going on down there?"

"You know we were able to replace all the U.S. Border patrol with our own Texas Patrol, a couple years ago, when the Federal Government didn't protect our citizens from the cartel gangs. I just want to make sure they're all set with enough men to patrol the 18 checkpoints along the border.

"Then I need to stop by and check-in with General Snead at Lackland. We're gonna need air support from them on Friday. And to tell you the truth, I miss my wife. I'm gonna have her meet me in San Antonio for dinner."

"Yes sir, I'll go take care of that right away."

"Oh lieutenant, bring your wives down as

well. You guys haven't been home for a while."

"Yes sir," said Stephens with a smile."

"Colonel Bowie, we just got word, Captain Cormac needs to see you at headquarters."

"Tell him I'll be right there. Well, gentlemen, if you all are done, let's go see what the Captain wants."

* * * * *

The sun was only a few feet off the Eastern horizon as the Colonel and his entourage walked the thirty yards to the old motel office. It was a dry, dusty, thirty-eight degree, January morning and the wind forced the Colonel to flip up his collar. In front of the motel sat a group of U.S. Marines with their hands zip tied behind their backs.

"What do we have Captain?"

"Colonel, these seventeen men were caught sneaking across the border early this morning. They all claim to be Texans and want to join the cause."

"Who's in charge here?"

"I am sir. Corporal Lewis Dear at your service," said the young Marine jumping to his feet.

"Corporal, I'm Colonel James Bowie. Why should I trust you? How do I know you're not gonna spy on us?"

"Colonel Sir we're all Texans and we love our Republic and we don't like what's happening in the rest of the country. I was a private under your command when you retired, sir. My namesake fought at the Alamo side by side yours."

"Who would your namesake be? I don't remember any Dears on the list."

"Sir, my full name is Lewis Dewall Dear."

"Lewis Dewall you say. What rank was he and where did he hail from?"

"Sir, he was a private and was born in Manhattan, New York."

"If he was from New York, how did you end up in Texas?"

"Sir, his wife, still carrying his son, came to Texas with him. She lived up in the Dallas area while he went down to fight, his son was born two days after the Alamo fell. She stayed after the war and married a guy named Dear. It's quite a story."

"What about the rest of these Marines?"

"Sir, they're all Texans. You know we tend to congregate when we're away from the Lone Star State. They want to be part of the Republic and involved in setting ourselves free."

"Captain, get these men into our uniforms and send them over to the Arkansas border. They shouldn't have to fight their friends in the 3/7.

Corporal Dear is staying with me."

"Yes sir, right away."

"Colonel, are you sure you want this guy with us? Lieutenant Stephens, quietly asked. "We really don't know much about him."

"I'm positive. Find him a sergeants uniform and the weapon of his choosing. We need to get going so make it snappy."

"Yes sir. Come on corporal let's get you the correct duds. It looks like you've been promoted to sergeant. What kind of weapon do you prefer?"

"Yes sir! I prefer the M-4 Carbine with a grenade launcher, Sir"

"Sergeant Dear, I heard that," said Bowie. "You won't need the grenade launcher. You'll be my sergeant until Sergeant Major Lazier gets here."

"The Sergeant Major Lazier, Sir? He's a legend in the 3/7."

"Yes Dear – Oh man, I'm gonna have to come up with a different name for you. I only call my wife 'dear'. What'd you say your first name was?"

"Sir, Lewis, Sir. You're not the first that wanted to change it," he said with a smile.

"Okay. Lieutenant get things done."

"Yes Sir."

Chapter Fifteen

The drive to the airstrip took about fifteen minutes. Sergeant Dear, drove with Lieutenant Stephens in the passenger seat and Colonel Bowie in the back of the SUV. The rest of his security team followed in a Humvee. The Colonel's plane was a twin turboprop, Fairchild Metro, capable of handling up to 22 passengers in a stripped down version. Colonel Bowie's was far from stripped down and carried no more than twelve very comfortably.

"Not a bad ride is it Sergeant?"

"Sir, yes sir."

"Listen Lewis, when it's just us," he said waving his arms at the Texas Rangers. "Just call me Colonel. Not so many Marine 'sir, yes sirs'. Got that?"

"Sir, yes Sir – I mean okay Colonel. Where

are we off to Colonel?"

"That's on a need to know basis and I don't think you need to know yet. I'll get more open after I've had a chance to feel you out Sergeant."

"Understood Sir."

"You must've gotten up pretty early this morning to cross the border. Why don't you get some rest we'll be in the air for a couple hours."

* * * * *

The twin turboprop landed in San Antonio an hour and a half later. Colonel Bowie and his security team drove to the Border Patrol Headquarters. One of Governor Bent's first moves after his reelection was to take over the Mexican-Texas border patrol. The Federal bureaucracy had allowed illegal aliens to cross the border to easily. The drug cartels had all but overtaken the smaller Texas towns along the border. The battle against the cartels was bloody, but one town after another was set free under the Governor's protection. The whole border was now physically protected by an elite, military trained, border patrol thanks to the efforts of Lieutenant Colonel William F. Hadley, Marine Corp retired.

"Hey Bill, how's the border look?" Bowie

asked as he walked into headquarters.

"James, it's so good to see you again," he said throwing his arms around his friend.

"Yeah, what's it been, a little over a year since I consulted with you?"

Colonel Bowie and Lt. Colonel Hadley set up the training of the new 20,000 member Texas Border Patrol. Each patrol officer was required to spend 4 months in one of the most rigid and toughest boot training camps. State of the art weaponry and electronic equipment was at the disposal of these elite fighting men. Mexican drug cartels didn't have a chance in hell against the capabilities of the Texas Mounted Guards.

"What brings you down here, James? You've got your hands full up North. We've got this end covered."

"I know ya do. I just wanted to talk a little strategy with you," said Bowie walking over to the map of the border area. "Do you think we can move some men from this eastern section up closer to New Mexico? I would like to have them swing north up the New Mexico border say about 50 miles."

"We can do that. It's been real quiet up and down the grid. We've already got a small unit working that area. The illegals jump across in New

Mexico, head north a few miles then cross over into Texas."

"Unfortunately, I think the U.S. is gonna try to bring in some saboteurs and assassins to take out our leadership. I need your men to keep them out. No one comes through without a Texas ID."

"Will do Colonel. Can you sit down for a cup of coffee? I'll fill you in on how we licked the drug gangs."

"Thanks Bill. I'd love to but I just don't have the time today. I'm heading up to Lackland to make sure we're gonna have air support when the time comes. Keep the faith Bill," he said holding out his arms for a hug and pat on the back.

"You too brother."

* * * * *

Lackland AFB, once the Gateway to the Air Force, was closed during the 2014 restructuring of the U.S. Military. All military units once assigned to the base were either closed down or moved to the Kirkland AFB in Albuquerque, New Mexico. The base was home to the the Republic of Texas Air Force, formerly the Texas Air National Guard, under the command of General Thomas Snead.

General Snead was born and reared in San

Antonio. He had come up through the ranks of the Guard after he graduated from the University of Texas.

"Colonel Bowie, welcome to our facilities," said Master Sergeant Kelly. "The General is expecting you, go right in."

"Thank you Sergeant, make sure my men get what they need," he said nodding at Sergeant Dear and the Rangers.

"Yes sir."

"Hello General Snead, how are the preparations going?"

"Right down to business, hey Colonel?"

"I'm sorry Tom, it's been a busy couple of months and it's all coming down to the wire. I'm trying to touch base with everyone before all hell breaks lose on Friday."

"You think Friday's the day?"

"Yeah, yesterday at 1:00 PM. they gave us seventy-two hours to surrender or be invaded. Here's what we've got." Walking over to the wall map of Texas and pointing out where the enemy troops were located, he continued. "We'll shut down the Amarillo airport all day Friday for your use. Every fifteen minutes I would like a flyover along the border here," he said, pointing to the border along New Mexico. "We need to let these young

Marines know we've got air support. Make sure each bird shows off the Yellow Rose of Texas."

"We finished painting the last one yesterday afternoon. I must say they are sharp looking. Would you like to take a look?" He asked reaching for his cap.

"That depends on whether my wife has arrived or not."

"Actually, I think all the wives are here. They're over at the officers club having a late lunch with my wife."

"Well then, I would rather see my sharp looking wife, if you don't mind."

"I understand. Why don't we head on over to the club."

"Sounds good to me. Can you make sure my Sergeant and the single Rangers get settled?"

"Sergeant Kelly should already have that taken care of. He's a sharp young man. Best Master Sergeant I've ever had."

Chapter Sixteen

Colonel Bowie paused as he entered the Officers Club and waited for his eyes to adjust to the darkness. Once his pupils opened he turned his head to find his wife sitting with five other ladies in the back corner. His gaze caught her gaze and for a split second they soaked each other in before she got up and came toward him. They met somewhere in the middle and he swept her up in his arms.

"Baby, I've missed you," he said giving her a squeeze and a kiss. "It's been too long."

"Tell me about it! I missed you too Honey. Have you had anything to eat? They have a great bacon cheeseburger."

"I could go for one. Looks like these Texas Rangers missed their better halves as well. Okay guys, listen up. I don't need any security while we're on the base so enjoy your time. The General's

Sergeant has you all set up in the officers quarters. We leave at seven in the morning. Try to get a little sleep before then," Looking at his wife he said. "Let's get that burger to go, okay?"

"Yes sir, honey bear," she said quietly as she rubbed his back and stole another kiss.

* * * * *

"Man, these Air Force jocks sure have some nice quarters. They make our old Marine apartments look like slums," Bowie said as he threw his bag on the floor.

"I know I was really excited when I saw it. I expected the drab olive green worn out look. Oh I missed you," Malinda said throwing her arms around her man knocking him back onto the bed. They both rolled over as they kissed.

James held her face in his hands and said. "Mal, I've got to be out of here early and I don't know how long it'll be before we see each other again. I hate not being close to you."

"I feel the same way James," pulling his head down as their lips touched.

"Baby, hold that thought, I've gotta take a shower it's been a long day," he said slowly getting out of the bed.

"Okay, go ahead," she said pushing him with her feet playfully. "I'll get some fresh clothes out of your bag for you to get into when you're done."

"I'm not planning on putting clothes on," he said with a sly grin.

James was in the process of rinsing off his hair when he heard the shower door sliding open and a soft pair of hands caressing his chest. Turning he met his wife's lips with his.

* * * * *

With her head calmly resting on James' chest, Malinda brought up the subject that had slipped to the back of their minds for the past forty minutes.

"Honey, how do you think this is all going to work out?"

Stroking her long auburn hair he said. "I'm hoping they will back down on their threat before Friday. If not, there's gonna be an all out war and Texas is gonna be a battleground. I don't think we'll invade the USA but we will protect our borders to the end."

"This is gonna be worse than your deployments to Afghanistan isn't it?" She said, tearing up.

"I'm afraid it could be another civil war. There are a lot of Texans who live in other States and a lot of them in the military."

"Oh Honey, are you gonna be all right? I don't think I could bear to live without you."

"Hey come on now. This is supposed to be good time for us," he said rolling her off his chest and on to her back and planting a long romantic kiss.

"Ooh you really did miss me."

"Baby, next to the Lord, you are my life."

"And I'd have it no other way dear." She reached over turned off the lights and wrapped herself in his arms for one last night together.

* * * * *

The knock on the door startled the, still wrapped up, lovebirds awake. "Five-thirty, Colonel, time to get up," came a yell from the other side.

"I've got to get ready. You gonna come to breakfast with me?"

"Yeah, but hold me for a bit more."

"With pleasure babe," wrapping his arms around his beautiful wife and pulling her close he said. "I love you."

"Hmm, the feeling's mutual lover."

Fifteen minutes later James got up and jumped in the shower. He was a little disappointed that he didn't get a visitor this time. Yet, he also knew he had to be ready to fly out by seven.

Chapter Seventeen

"Vice President Brody to see you sir."

"Send him in Delores."

"Hello Mr. President," said the VP holding out his hand.

"Hello Adam, have a seat."

After shaking with the president, Brody sat on the edge of a wing chair with his hands interlocked in a nervous fashion.

"What's up Adam? You look a little tense."

"I just talked with Vice President Chandler, she's trying to set up a meeting between you and President Watson. She's against war and is hoping the two of you can work things out or at least begin some talks to slow things down."

"Did Watson approve that?"

"I'm not sure she's touched base with him yet. She wanted me to talk with you first."

"I think some talking would be good. No one wants to see a war between the States. But he's gonna have to give some respect to the Republic."

"I suggest that you meet with him in a neutral State like Louisiana. I doubt he would come here and you should definitely not go there."

"Sounds good. It's just after one on Wednesday, so we have less than forty-eight hours. See if you can get it set for early tomorrow morning."

"I'll give her a call right away sir. How's Lake Charles sound for the meet?"

"That sounds good I'll give their governor a call and send some Rangers over to get a secure location."

"Delores, have Lieutenant Tucker report to my office."

"Yes sir, right away, he's just out in the hallway."

"Lieutenant, I need you to take a few men and set up a secure location in Lake Charles, Louisiana. President Watson and I may be holding some peace talks tomorrow morning. Keep in contact with Vice President Brody for details."

"Yes sir. What mode of transportation do you want?"

"You're the expert, set up what you think is

best."

"Yes sir, Mr. President."

"Lieutenant, this is a needs to know basis."

Giving a nod of his head the lieutenant turned and walked out.

"Delores, get me Governor Rickert on the phone please."

"Mr. President."

"Yes Delores."

"The Governor was not available. He'll call back as soon as he can."

"Thank you. Delores, I need fifteen minutes of quiet so hold all my calls except for the Governor."

President Bent stood up, took a big drink of water, and walked around the desk to the wing chair Brody had used. Kneeling, he placed his elbows on the seat, intertwined his hands and rested his forehead upon them.

"My most gracious Heavenly Father. I ask of You, no I beg You to make this meeting happen. You know my heart, Father. I don't want to see anyone, on either side, killed in a war. You are the omnipotent One, You have the power to put a stop to this. Give me the words to say that could defuse the situation and soften President Watson's heart for You. What a difference it could make if he would trust Jesus as his Lord and Savior. Father, Your Word tells us that You are the God of the impossible.

"Lord, help me to be open to Your leading each step of the way. I believe, with all my heart, this secession is what You would have for us in Texas. That You want to be recognized as the Creator of heaven and earth and we, the United States, have worshiped the creature rather than You.

"Now the President wants to take You completely out of the picture. Oh Lord, turn us back to You. Use Texas to show the world Your power and might. May Your light shine so bright on the shores and borders of Texas that the world will know who we serve.

"Father once again I pray for this meeting to . . ."

"Mr. President, it's Governor Rickert on line one."

". . . Happen. I ask these things in the name of Jesus. Amen." Walking over to his desk and picking up the phone. "Hello Governor, I've got a favor to ask of you."

"Ask away, Halford."

"We're trying to set up a peace talk meeting with President Watson and would like it to be in Lake Charles."

"I was on the phone with President Watson when you called earlier. Apparently they want the same thing for tomorrow morning around ten."

"Thank you Lord," Bent said under his breath.

"What was that, Halford?"

"I said 'thank you Lord'. I've got some of my Rangers heading your way to secure the area. Where's it gonna be?"

"We're working on the Lakehills Suites. It's located right off of I-210 about six miles from the regional airport."

"Okay, I'll have them meet your team there. Thanks for letting us hold this in your State."

"No problem. Listen Halford, if this works out and Texas is allowed to secede, we may want to look at annexation."

"Let's take one step at a time and keep that quiet. If Watson thinks he'll lose more States we won't have any peace treaty. Thanks again Governor."

"You're welcome and we will be praying for you all."

"Mr. President, Vice President Brody is waiting to see you."

"Send him in."

"Hal, I just got off the phone with Vice

113

President Chandler, Watson said he will meet with you," he said with an air of excitement.

"Yeah, I know. I just got off the phone with Governor Rickert. It's all set up in Lake Charles."

"Man, I sure hope you two can work something out. My wife's family's from New York and they're giving her a hard time. She's the only conservative one in the bunch. This is pitting family against family."

"Tell me about it. I've got a nephew in the U.S. Army and another serving as a pilot aboard that aircraft carrier that just entered the Gulf. My sister in New Hampshire is having a fit," he said shaking his head. "I'm gonna spend the night in Beaumont so we can drive to the meeting in the morning. Its only about fifty miles to Lake Charles from there."

"You gonna stay at the Beaumont Inn? Mrs. Herbert sure can put on the feed bag. My wife loves the place."

"So does Alyssa. I thought it would be nice to get away with her even if it is just for a few hours."

Chapter Eighteen

The Beaumont Inn, a small bed and
breakfast, came to life as President and Mrs. Bent
came down to the breakfast table. Laid out before
them was a meal fit for a king. Small bowls of
cantaloupe and watermelon placed next to tall
glasses of orange juice and a pot full of strong black
coffee were sitting in the breakfast nook
overlooking the backyard garden.

President Bent reached across the table and
took Alyssa's hands into his as they bowed in prayer
for the provisions the Lord had provided. After the
prayer he looked into her eyes and mouthed the
words, "I love you."

She smiled back and with a voice that all
could hear said, "I love you to, husband and I pray
the Lord's blessing on you all this morning."

"Thank you Alyssa, God hears your prayers

I think more than mine."

"Hal, you know better than that."

"You know what I mean," he said as the host set a plate of eggs Benedict in front of him. "You always have the best food, Mrs Herbert"

"Why thank you kindly, Governor. Oh, I should have called you Mr. President. I'm so sorry."

"That's okay. It's been kinda hard for it to sink into my head as well. Wasn't what I expected when I took office."

"Is there anything else I can get you two before I serve your men?"

"I think we're fine Mrs. Herbert. Thank you," he said smiling.

President Bent and Alyssa quietly discussed the future of their two children as they ate the wonderful breakfast.

"What do you think will happen to Billy and Cloe should Texas lose the bid to be it's own country."

"Alyssa, I fear for them regardless if we win or lose. The world has gotten awful dark the last few years. I hope they keep their focus on the Lord through it all. Which is exactly what we need to do," he said taking his last sip of coffee.

"Mr. President, we need to be heading out in about fifteen minutes. It's a fifty-four mile drive to

Lake Charles and we should allow an hour and a half to get there," Lieutenant Tucker said from the doorway.

"I'm ready when you are Lieutenant."

Getting up from his seat he reached over and helped Alyssa to her feet. Sweeping her into his arms he gave her a passionate hug and kiss. "Are you ready to go? You heard the Ranger, we leave in fifteen."

"I'll be ready. I will need your charge card. I'm gonna spend the day shopping at the Lake Charles Mall."

"I should have known," he said with a smile.

* * * * *

"Sir, we'll be pulling up at the Lakehills Suites in about five minutes," Tucker said as they pulled off the interstate onto the service road.

"Good, I'll have some time to freshen up before the meeting. I need two of the men to go with my wife to the mall. If they keep a low profile no one will know how important she is to me."

Patting her hand he leaned over and gave her a kiss goodbye. "Keep your eyes open. The Rangers will be close the whole time but you still need to be aware of your surroundings."

"Don't worry about me. You just concentrate on making peace with President Watson," she said returning his kiss. "I have faith in you dear."

As the caravan pulled up to the suites. Two Texas Rangers came out and one opened the rear door to the black SUV. "Good morning Mr. President you're the first to arrive. The group of rooms is just past the front desk to the right."

"Good morning Rangers," he said sticking his head back through the open door giving his wife another kiss. "Don't buy out the store, honey."

"Go get ready for your meeting," she responded smiling. "I'll be praying for the Lord's will."

President Bent closed the door and watched as the SUV with his wife and two Texas Rangers pulled away. He threw her a kiss and walked into the hotel.

* * * * *

At precisely ten o'clock, Halford Abbot Bent, walked into the meeting room and quickly greeted President Watson with a nod and handshake. He received the same back. Glancing around the room he noticed a refreshment area with coffee, water and donuts, a white board on the east wall and a computer terminal where the transcriber was sitting. A Secret Service agent was standing in the north corner carefully watching Lieutenant Tucker who had taken a position just inside the door.

The conference table was approximately six feet by two and a half feet with each president sitting face to face across the table.

"Mr. President, I assume I'll get a copy of the record your man is taking."

"Yes you will Gov . . . oh excuse me you want to be called President Bent."

"Thank you. If you don't mind can we go by first names?"

"That's okay with me Halford, call me Nick."

"And I go by Hal."

"Well, Hal, I think we're off to a good start. Unfortunately, I'm afraid its gonna get rocky. You do realize that you don't have the power or the legal rights to leave the Union."

"I would beg to differ with you. It's gonna come down to how we interpret the laws and our constitutions. The Declaration of Independence clearly states, *"the people have the right to alter their government in such manner as they might think proper."* The Texas Constitution, both our original and the current, states the same thing."

"Hal, the Civil war proved that States cannot secede the Union. The Union won that war showing the illegal act of secession."

"Nick, all that did was show that the stronger military wins. It did nothing to prove morality or legality of secession."

"When you combine the Civil War with the U.S. Supreme court ruing of *Texas vs. White*, it's obvious that it is illegal."

The *Texas vs. White* Supreme court case, in 1869, involved the legality of United States bonds owned by Texas and purchased by George W. White and John Chiles. In accepting original jurisdiction, the Supreme Court ruled that Texas had remained a state and had never left the Union.

"Nick, if that were the case then why did President Grant have to sign a Re-admittance Act to allow Texas back into the Union in the early 1870's? If they had never left they wouldn't need to be re-admitted."

"Hal, you were right, it is going to come down to interpretation of the laws. Bottom line is, Texas is a part of the United States and it is gonna stay a part of the Union. We are mightier than you and we will win the war."

"President Watson, there is no law that

forbids a state to withdraw from the Union. Texas was a country when we voluntarily joined the United States of America and now that we have voluntarily withdrawn we are a sovereign country free from your rule," Bent said calmly. "We are seceding and we would like to do it peaceably with no life lost. I am asking you to withdraw your deadline to invade the Republic of Texas."

Putting his hands on the table, standing and leaning over the inches from Bent's face he angrily said, "You will lose this war. I will not allow you or anyone else to tell me how to run this country. Friday at one, we cross the border. Stand down or die."

"Well, it looks like we are at an impasse. Please pray about it and come to a better decision."

"PRAY! I don't believe in your God. I believe in the human intellect and reason. You can pray all you want but we are stronger than you or your God.," cried Watson slamming back into his chair.

"Thank you for your time President Watson," he said standing and holding out his hand.

Slapping his hand away, he responded, "Get outta here and watch your back."

"I'm sorry we couldn't work something out," Bent said as he walked out.

Watson looked over at the transcriber, "Get out of here and make that transcript sound like he was the bastard."

"Yes sir, Mr. President."

"You to," he said to the agent.

As soon as the door closed behind him Watson made a call. "It's a go."

Chapter Nineteen

"Let's go," commanded President Bent as he came out of Lakehills with his phone to his ear. "Alyssa, we're on our way, meet us on the service road. Love you."

"Things didn't go well, Mr. President. Watson's not right in the head."

"Lieutenant, show respect. That would be President Watson's not right in the head."

"Yes sir, Mr. President," Tucker said chuckling.

"I think we're in for quite a battle. Let's get my wife and head back home. I don't think we're safe out of Texas."

"We're on it sir."

Five minutes later they were picking up Alyssa Bent. Two Texas Rangers were in the lead car, Lieutenant Tucker, Ranger Witt, President Bent and his wife in the middle vehicle and two more Rangers following in a third. As the caravan headed up the West bound ramp to I-210 they picked up speed in an effort to get home quickly.

"Okay pretty lady, let's see what you bought?"

Opening the bag she moved it to where he could see inside and whispered, "It's a sexy nightie for later tonight at the Bed and Breakfast," she said with a twinkle in her eyes.

"Oh baby, I'm sorry, but we're gonna have to head back to Austin tonight. Things didn't go very well and I've got a lot of planning to do." Peering into the bag, he let out a quiet whistle, "It sure does look interesting."

"Bummer, I was hoping for another special night in Beaumont."

"Me too Alyssa, me too."

"The nice part about this nightie is that it will work wherever we are, as long as we're together."

"Unfortunately, I'm sure I'll be coming to bed late tonight."

"That's okay honey, I'll wait up for you," She said with a crooked smile.

"You're so good to me. How did I ever deserve someone like you."

Alyssa snuggled up close to her husband as he laid a kiss on her head. For the next forty minutes they quietly held each other.

"Mr. President we're coming up to the Texas roadblock. We'll be back home in a few minutes."

Sitting up and looking around he said, "Lieutenant, this roadblock is a mile or more from our border. Something's not right."

"Witt, slow up while I call the lead car."

The two Rangers in the first car had already arrived at the checkpoint when they answered their phone. "What can I do for you Lieutenant?"

"We're slowing down something doesn't look right up there. We're still in Louisiana, the checkpoint should be up the road."

"Okay, we'll check it out," he said rolling down his window to talk with the guard on the passenger side. "Corporal, why isn't this roadblock in Texas?"

"Because we aren't Texans. They made us, Randy," he said as he put a round into the Ranger's head.

Randy did the same to the driver and a military Humvee pulled out from behind the makeshift guard house headed toward the rest of the caravan.

"Get us the hell out of here," Tucker yelled.

Witt hit the gas and headed off road into the field followed closely by the third vehicle. The Humvee sped toward them with the mini-gun blazing. Witt knew they could outrun the heavier armored Humvee and only had about a mile to the Texas border. With the rough terrain accurate shooting was next to impossible. Bullets ripped through the rear vehicle like it was butter. Before they could get out of range the trailing black SUV exploded into a ball of flame.

"Oh no," Alyssa cried putting her hand over her mouth.

"keep your head down," said Bent as he pulled her down.

A host of bullets ripped through the car as they drove out of range and back onto I-210. Lieutenant Tucker had already called for help and half a dozen Texas Hummers surrounded them and lead them safely back into friendly territory.

"Mr. President, are you and your wife hurt?"

"I caught some shrapnel in my side. Alyssa are you okay?" He asked as he moved from his protective location on top of her. "Alyssa! She's been shot. We need a medic!"

Lieutenant Tucker jumped over the front seat as Witt rushed to the Beaumont hospital.

President Bent and Tucker worked at getting

the bleeding stopped. With Alyssa's head in his lap and tears running down his cheeks Bent said, "He has just made the biggest mistake of his life."

"Who's that Mr. President?" Tucker asked.

"Watson that's who, he's gonna pay for this. Those were U.S. Special Forces and I have no doubt they were sent by him."

Tucker was surprised by the uncharacteristic anger and hatred he heard in the President's voice. The usually mild mannered man was visibly shaken.

* * * * *

Texas Rangers Tucker and Witt both stood as the President walked into the waiting room.

"How's your side sir?" Witt asked.

"I'll be okay. You did some great driving out there. What have you heard about the other four Rangers?"

Shaking his head Tucker responded. "All dead, sir. The Captain's gonna notify their families. What about your wife?"

"She's in surgery. Somebody will come out when they know something. I'm gonna go into the consultation room for a word of prayer."

"Yes sir."

"My gracious Heavenly Father, I believe

that I'm doing the right thing here in Texas. I know that you are in control and I trust you through it all. But Lord, why Alyssa? She was just along for the ride. Why her?" Sobbing he continued, "Lord, give the doctors direction as they do the surgery, keep their hands steady. Be with the nurses and anesthetist, each one who is caring for her.

"Father, I don't know what I would do without her. Next to You, she is my life. Watch over her and bring her through this with little or no damage to her physical body. I know we will both grow closer to You as we deal with this circumstance. Father, please, I beg of You to bring my dear wife through this. Don't let her die and . . ."

"Mr. President, the doctor is here with news," Tucker said knocking on the door.

"Getting up from his kneeling position Bent said. "Please, send him in."

"Hello, Mr. President. I'm Doctor Gordon."

"Doctor," he said reaching out his hand. "Lieutenant Tucker would you join us."

Tucker walked in pulling the door closed behind him. Doctor Gordon motioned for them to take a seat as he sat at the table.

"How is she? Is she going to make it?"

"She is holding her own but in guarded condition. The bullet passed through like this," the doctor began to draw a quick picture of the abdomen and with a line showing the travel of the bullet as he spoke. "It entered just below her left breast, continued down and missed all her vital organs and exited out her right thigh. It is a miracle that it missed all of the large blood vessels. She would have bled out in minutes if it had nicked even one of them."

"Thank you God," said the President briefly looking up.

"I'll agree with you, President Bent, she should be dead. Somebody's up there's looking out for you both."

"It's not just somebody. It's God Almighty. Go on Doctor Gordon."

"The bad news is that the bullet did gaze the colon," holding up his index finger of his left hand he pointed with his other. "The bullet ran directly along the colon like this," moving his finger from the knuckle to the tip of the finger. "Like a sharp knife it cut the colon and the toxins spilled out. Most of the surgery was stitching it back up and cleaning out the poisons that filled the cavity."

"How long will the recovery be?"

"I can't tell you that. We'll have to keep a close eye on her for the next couple of weeks. Infection is our main concern. It is very hard to

129

make sure we got it all cleaned up."

"Can she be moved to Austin" Lieutenant Tucker asked.

"Let's wait a few days to see how she's doing. I'd like to have her fully awake before any attempts are made to move her."

"Thank you Doctor Gordon," said President Bent as he stood holding out his hand.

"You're welcome. Mr. President, politically I disagree with the direction you're taking Texas but rest assured we will take excellent care of your wife."

"Thank you. I trust your medical ability. However, after what President Watson just ordered you still think I'm making a bad choice?"

"President Bent, are you positive that he ordered this ambush?"

"I have no doubt, even if I don't have the proof yet," he said walking out the door.

Chapter Twenty

Sautee Nachoochee, Georgia, was especially quiet when Robert, Sally and Joe came through on Main Street. The plan was to fill up both vehicles at different stations. Josh and Addi had pulled into the first one they found open on the outskirts of town. The cold winter wind bit on his neck and cheeks, as Josh lifted his jacket collar and began to fill up the Jeep.

"Addi, if you need to use the restroom do it now. I got a feeling that there's not gonna be a lot of places open this time of year."

"Okay Honey," she said opening her door. "You want anything to munch on or a drink?"

"Naw. We're gonna stop on the other side of town and have some of the sandwiches you and Sally packed. I'll wait until then."

"I'll be right back."

"Hey, I think I will have a coke," he yelled as she opened the door to the station.

Waving to him, she walked into the small convenience store and gas station. Glancing around for the bathroom, she noticed an older woman look up from behind the cash register. Before Addi could get the words out, the woman pointed to the sign in the back corner. Addi gave her a flip of the hand and mouthed the words "Thank you."

She walked out of the restroom and grabbed a bottle of coke and a water for herself. Patting her stomach her thoughts went to her unborn baby. *This one doesn't need any caffeine.*

"That'll be $3.98. How far along are you, sweetie?" The store clerk asked.

"Only a couple of months," she said as she handed her $4.00. "Just put the Two cents into the little cup."

"Sure thing sweetie. I'm sure glad I've already raised my kids. I wouldn't wanna bring kids up in this crazy mixed up world. I was just reading the paper and the Feds are taking away people's citizenship because they signed some petition thingy. Can you believe that?"

"Oh really, I haven't heard about that," she said as she looked down at the sodas.

"You haven't heard," she said noticeably

startled. "Where you been Sweetie? It's all over the news."

"My husband and I have been on the road the last couple of days. You have a nice day ma'am."

"You too Sweetie and tell that man to treat you and the baby right, ya hear."

Josh had just hung the nozzle back on the tank when she got to the Jeep. "Hey Baby, let me get that for you," he said rushing around to get the door. "How're you and our bundle of joy doing? he asked helping her in.

"We're okay," she said leaning over to give him a kiss. "We better get a move on, if we're gonna meet with the others."

"I think I'm gonna pull up near the building and see if I can pick up a wireless signal. I want to see if there's any news about us."

Pulling up to the south side of the garage, out of site of the front windows, he grabbed his laptop. Addi marveled every time he opened his machine. One quick flip and he had it open, turned on and clicking his fingers waiting for it to boot up.

"Cool, I've got a connection. Let's see what's going on in our world," he said as he clicked on his favorite national news site and began scanning the headlines. "Hey, Watson and Bent are meeting right now trying to work things out. Maybe things won't escalate any further."

"Oh, I hope they can come up with an agreement. Any update on those of us who've signed the petitions?"

"Yeah, it looks like they're still being picked up. Looks like a lot of folks are in an uproar because family members are being sent to detention camps," he said shaking his head in disgust. "I'm thinking we don't want to get caught. We need to head out and meet up with the rest and fill them in," Josh said closing the laptop.

* * * * *

Robert and Sally went into the market as Joe pumped gas. Robert notice a local sheriff parked across the street talking to someone on his cell phone. He did not appear to be paying attention to the out of state minivan.

"Let's get what we need and get outta here," Robert whispered to Sally. "A deputy is parked over there and I don't want him getting suspicious."

"Where," she said turning her head.

"Don't look, just take my word for it, he's there. Use the restroom and I'll grab us something to drink and pay for the gas."

By the time Joe finished filling the van, Robert was up at the counter waiting to pay.

"I'm paying for that gas out there."

"The gas is $84 and the three drinks are $5.97 for a total off $89.97."

"Six bucks a gallon for gas is ridiculous. Do you remember when it was like a dollar and a quarter?"

"Yes sir I do. It wasn't all that long ago was it? I heard they're slapping another tax on it next week. I guess the plan is to build the military back up since Texas decided to skip out," said the clerk shaking his head.

"It's a little late. They shouldn't have cut it in the first place. There's no way they can build it up quick enough now. Thanks for the gas."

"No thank you! We don't get a lot of customers this time of year. I barely make enough to stay open during the winter months."

Walking to the van, Robert was relieved that the sheriff's car was gone. He wrapped his arm around his lovely wife and pulled her close. Looking up at him and straining her neck she gave him a big kiss and said. "I will always love you."

He smiled and opened the sliding side door and helped her in. "Hey Joe, if you're ready for a break, I'll drive."

"These old bones are getting a little stiff. I just saw Josh and Addi drive by. I'll try to get them on the walkie talkies."

"Good, tell them to look for a meeting spot about ten minutes outside of town. Did you see that cop car when we pulled in?"

"Yeah. I was glad when he took off. Hope he didn't see our plates."

"I think he would've called for back-up if he saw them. There's gotta be an APB out on us."

Chapter Twenty-One

"We're about ten miles outside of town at a little rest area," Josh called on the walkie talkies. "Right hand side of the road. It's got a couple of picnic tables and old outhouses."

"Okay. We'll be there in a couple of minutes," Robert replied.

The minivan pulled up next to Josh's Jeep and all five went down a small hill to a picnic table sheltered from the wind by a bank of pine trees. Sally set a basket full of sandwiches and chips in the center of the table and Robert asked a blessing for the food.

"Hey guys, I was able to get an Internet connection at the gas station. Watson and Bent were involved in a peace talk of some sort today."

"No kidding. What happened?" Sally asked.

"I don't know. I guess they're still at it.

Although, they're still looking for non-citizens so the hunt for us is still on. We need to be careful. I don't want my baby born in some detention camp."

The sound of tires on gravel turned their heads up to the road.

"Oh great," Robert said as the deputy pulled up behind his van. "I was hoping he would've stayed closer to town. Looks like he's running our plates. I assume he'll just stay up there until back-up comes."

"What should we do? How we gonna get out of here? Honey, I don't want to kill anyone," Sally said as she watched Robert feel for his gun.

"Sally, calm down. We'll play it by ear. Let's just wait and see what he does. Eat your sandwiches and pretend every thing's okay. Josh and Addi, slide down to the other end of the table and make like we just met."

Getting out of his car, the deputy positioned his hat and walked to the back of the vehicle. He kept his eyes on the five as he opened the trunk and pulled out a shotgun. Slamming the trunk shut he turned and slowly walked toward them.

"Something's not right," Robert said soaking in the situation. "If he knew who we were, he'd wait for back-up. Don't do anything rash and let me do the talking. Joe head over to the van and see what he does."

Joe began to walk up the small hill twenty feet to the left of the officer.

"You come back here," said the deputy motioning to Joe.

"I'm just going up to the van."

"No, you're not. Come on," he said motioning again.

Looking back to Robert, he was given the nod to come back.

"What can we do for you officer?" Robert asked.

"What are you folks doing in the fine State of Georgia?"

Pointing to Josh and Addi he said, "I don't know about those two but the three of us are just passing through."

"You're not together?" He asked looking over at Josh.

"No, we just met them here. We were here first and they just came and joined us. Never saw them before," Josh said.

"That's interesting. Why did you beep and wave when you passed them at the gas station?"

"Um, um, because they were the only ones in the whole town."

"Okay. Like I really believe that," the

officer said with a bit of sarcasm. "Sergeant Major, it's been a while. How have you been?"

"Do I know you son?" Robert asked startled.

"Probably not. You had over eight hundred men under your command. I was just a lowly PFC and it has been a few years."

Robert looked down at the deputy's name badge. "PFC Carter, I remember you. Lima company, you handled the SAW."

The M249 Squad Automatic Weapon (SAW), also know as the Light Machine Gun, provided the Marines the ability to quickly gain and maintain fire superiority.

"Yes sir. What have you gotten yourself into?"

"We're just passing through, Officer Carter."

"I ran your tag, sir. There's a bolo that says you're headed east. When I heard your name I quickly told them I had made a mistake on the number. So they're still looking for you going east."

"Why'd you do that?"

"Well sir, I know whatever you did it had to be right. Ya don't get to be a Sergeant Major without a lot of good character. My assumption is that you lost your citizenship."

"Yep. Signed a secession petition and all hell broke lose."

"I figured as much," said Carter as an old pickup came to a stop. "That's my brother Blaine, Sergeant Major. He needs to get out of the area. He won't take a chip and won't last a day in a camp."

"What happened to his leg," said Robert watching Blaine heading their way with a limp.

"Lost it in Afghanistan in 2012. He was a Navy Seal and could come in handy for you. Blaine, this is Sergeant Major Robert Lazier. You've heard me talk about him."

"Yes I have. Good to meet you," he said holding out his hand.

Grabbing Blaine's hand Robert said, "Good to meet you to and thank you for giving of yourself for your country."

"Doesn't look like it did a lot of good. The administration has screwed us over big time. I barely got enough help to live. Now that I'm a man without a country I don't even get that."

"Well son. We're headed for Texas and you are welcome to come along."

"Thanks. I appreciate it. My old beater up there's not gonna make the trip. I'll need to ride with one of you."

"That's no problem we've got plenty of room. Josh ya got room for another?"

"Yeah, Addi and I could use some fresh

stories," he said reaching to shake Blaine's hand. "I'm Josh and this pretty lady is my wife Addison. Why don't you get your stuff and throw it in the Jeep."

"Good to meet you both," he said politely nodding to Addi. "I'll get my gear."

"Deputy Carter, can we talk over here for a minute?" Robert asked as he walk away.

"What's up sir?"

"You got a personal phone number where I can reach you. We might need some information from time to time. You would be a great undercover operator for us."

"Man, I'd love to do that. I would go with you myself, but I've got a wife and two kids under three. So whatever I can do to help I'm available."

"Great, and actually you'll be more help here than if you were with us. We need men we can trust on the inside."

"I'm not very far inside but I do have access to the police frequencies all over the country."

"Okay. We've got a ways to go so we're gonna head out. Been good to see you again, Marine."

Walking past the table and up the hill Robert motioned for the others to follow. Josh and Blaine had just finished loading Blaine's gear.

"You bring weapons with you?" Robert asked.

"Yeah, an M-16 and a couple of automatic pistols."

"Good, hopefully we won't need them but you never know. Everybody load up and let's hit the road."

Officer Carter and Blaine held a long hug as they said their goodbye.

Chapter Twenty-Two

"Your brother's a pretty cool guy. Letting us go and all," said Addi.

"Yeah, he's a great, big brother. Maybe a tad over protective but a great guy."

"Did you hear how the peace talks turned out?" Josh asked Blaine.

"Oh man, you haven't heard! President Bent was traveling back to Texas and they were ambushed by U.S. Special Forces."

"Was he killed?" Addi asked alarmingly.

"No, but he and his wife were both wounded. Four of his Texas Ranger security guards were killed."

"How bad are they?"

"Bent's was superficial but his wife is in serious condition. Yeah, they had a big press conference about forty-five minutes ago."

"So I would imagine it's all out war," Addi said.

"Yes Ma'am. President Watson's denying he had anything to do with it. Says it must have been a rogue unit upset with Texas trying to secede."

"Do you think that could be true?"

"No way. These guys take orders from someone else. They don't go off half-cocked. Somebody higher up gave them their orders. I gotta think it was Watson. Anyway, he's getting a lot of flack from all over the world. The United Nations is really ticked off at him. We've got some nasty protests taking place in New York and Washington. People are hot under the collar."

"Maybe that'll pressure President Watson into allowing Texas to secede," Josh said.

"Doesn't sound like he's gonna do that. He figures that if he gives in to Texas it'll start an avalanche of other States cutting the strings."

"I've gotta talk with Robert," Josh said shaking his head and reaching for the walkie talkie. "Can you hear me?"

"Load and clear. Whatcha need?"

"Hey Robert, Blaine was just telling us about President Bent getting ambushed. Four of his guys were killed and he and his wife were wounded. I guess the whole country's in an uproar. I'm gonna stop at the library in the next town and see what I can find out online."

"Okay, it looks like that'll be Cleveland, about twenty minutes down 75."

"Good. I can usually get a signal out in the parking lot. So we won't have to go in."

"Okay, when we get there bring your laptop to the van. We should all see what's going on together."

* * * * *

Josh turned into the Cleveland, Ga. library and found two open parking spots up front, close to the doors. Gathering his laptop, he, Addi and Blaine got out of the Jeep and quickly got in the van that had pulled up beside them. He set the computer up on the console and searched for an unsecured connection.

"Super, we are connected to the district library. Now to find the story," Josh said as he typed in 'Texas Governor ambush'. "Here's the newscast from earlier today."

"At approximately one this afternoon, The President of the New Republic of Texas was ambushed in western Louisiana, just outside the Texas border. Four Texas Ranger security guards where killed and President Bent and his wife Alyssa were wounded. We have little knowledge on their condition at this time. We believe they have crossed the border and are at a hospital in Beaumont, TX."

Scrolling across the bottom of the screen were the words, *Breaking News*. As the news caster said, "This just in. President Bent is holding a press conference at this very moment. We are switching over to our affiliate station, WAKC in Beaumont, TX."

"Ladies and Gentlemen of the press, citizens of the Republic of Texas, and to all who are listening both domestic and foreign," began President Bent. "My motorcade was ambushed by a team of U.S. Special Forces as we were returning from unsuccessful peace talks with Nicholas Watson, President of the United States of America.

"Four of my security team were innocently slaughtered in this attack. My wife, Alyssa, was seriously wounded and is in guarded condition at Beaumont General Hospital. She took a small arms bullet through her abdomen, piercing her intestines before exiting her right thigh. The doctors were able to repair the damage but she is in danger of major, life threatening infection," he said wiping a tear from his cheek. "Please be in prayer for her and for the wives and kids of the four Texas Rangers who were murdered."

Lifting his shirt and showing his bandages he continued. "I have a superficial shrapnel wound in my side which will heal up leaving only a small scar. I would like to thank the great doctors that performed the surgeries on myself and my wife. Without their quick action my wife would have been lost to me forever.

"I believe that this was a planned attack after the peace talks did not bring President Watson's desired outcome. Just in case you did not understand what I just said, let me be very clear. I believe this attack was ordered by the President of the United States. Innocent lives were lost and war has been declared on the people of Texas because Watson wants total power over his subjects.

"Good people of the United States, do not let this madman get away with destroying your great country and the freedoms you have enjoyed for the last 240 years.

"The People of Texas will fight to the death, just like we did at the Battle of the Alamo. We are committed to the cause of independence and will not tolerate our freedom to be taken away from us. If nothing else this attack reminds us, as Texans, to Remember the Alamo. We will be encouraged and reinforced by this unwarranted attack.

"It is not my desire to take lives in our struggle for sovereignty. However, I will not give in to tyranny. President Watson, if you must, bring it on. We will win or we will die trying.

"To all those in the USA who are listening – don't let him get away with stealing your freedom. Stand up for justice against senseless acts of violence from your Commander and Chief."

"Wow," said Joe. "That was a bold and moving speech. It ought to build up the Texas military."

"Wait there's more. A response from Watson."

"My fellow Americans, people of the State of Texas, I did not order a military strike on Halford Bent and his motorcade. This was no doubt perpetrated by a rogue Special Forces unit upset by Texas trying to pull out of the Union. I repeat I did not order the ambush. I am deeply saddened by the loss of life and the injuries caused to Mrs. Bent.

"I do not want war with Texas. I do, however, want Texas to remain a part of the United States. They do not have the right to secede and we will do what is necessary to keep them as a State even if that means using military force.

"The peace talks failed because Governor Bent was obstinate and mean spirited. He had no desire to find a compromise and threatened to destroy the United States of America any way he could. After it was obvious that we couldn't come to a mutual conclusion, I tried to leave on a peaceful note and he slapped my hand away, rather than shake it.

"It wouldn't surprise me that he set this whole ambush up himself to gain sympathy for his cause. He let it get out of control and wants to blame me for his actions.

"I did not order this ambush and if he wants war, we will give it to him. Governor Bent, or President, or whatever you want to be called, you have until Friday to withdraw your request for secession. At exactly one o'clock in the afternoon we will cross the Texas border and place you and your rebellious followers under military arrest."

"Wow and double wow! I can hardly believe where we've gone in like six days," Addi said.

"There is one good thing about this."

"What could that be, Blaine?" Interrupted Sally with a bewildered look.

"With all the uproar this is causing they will relax their search for us. They're gonna need their forces to put down the rioting. We may just make it to Texas without any interference."

"He's right about that. We've got about three

hours of daylight left. Let's hit the road and make good use of it."

Okay," Josh said. "What way we heading?

"Let's go South on 115 to 400 toward Atlanta. The we'll take the 285 bypass at Sandy Springs and jump on 20 West of Atlanta toward Alabama."

"I thought we were gonna stay on the back roads as much as possible?" Joe asked.

"I think we'll be okay now that this happened. Most of the patrolling police will be busy gearing up for riot control."

"Sounds good to me," Josh said. "We'll make better time. We should cross the Texas border in just over twelve hours if we drive straight through. Addi's gonna drive for us and I'll try to get connected via my cell phone. Maybe I can pick up on the repercussions of the ambush."

"Okay. Stay at least a half mile behind us," Robert said as he slid into the drivers seat of the minivan. "Let's git"

Chapter Twenty-Three

Heading South on 115, Blaine was catching up on some needed rest while Josh was busily hooking up his cell phone and laptop for an Internet connection.

"Honey, shouldn't you use one of the disposable phones?"

"Why would I do that when mine is still working? Besides, they don't have a data package with their service."

"What if the authorities are monitoring your phone? Won't they be able to track our location?"

"If they're following us I'm sure they could pin-point us with no problem. However, they don't know that we're with the Laziers. As far as I know, the police are after them not us."

"You know I'm computer illiterate so I trust your judgment. You're the techie not me."

"Hey, I'm connected. Now we'll be able to see what's happening. Let me see if I can stream in some conservative news and see what's really going on."

Wow! Josh thought to himself. Things are really happening. He half turned his computer away from Addi's eyes fearful that she might get upset about what he was viewing. "Hey honey, I'm gonna put on my head phones so I don't wake Blaine up or bother your driving."

"Okay, but I'm only gonna be good for about an hour. I'll need someone else to drive after that."

Nodding his head, Josh slipped on the head phones and began to watch video after video of martial law in action. Small groups of protesters had emerged because of the ambush against the Bent's and their security force. The local police forces were dispelling them as fast as they would gather.

Without warning, tear gas, billy clubs and fire hoses were being used on the helpless men and women who were voicing their concern. Constitutional rights had been thrown out the window in lieu of control by the military. In some of the major cities, where the protests were much larger, the National Guard had been called up and civil rights were being violated as the protests were put down with strong force.

The military was now in full control of services, legislature and courts. The Commander-in-Chief, President Watson, was now running everything with no checks and balances from the Senate or Congressional oversight. Roadblocks were up and running at every road leading into Texas. No one was allowed to enter.

Small detention camps were quickly erected at each roadblock for all those holding Texas drivers licenses and those who had their citizenship stripped and refused to take the chip. Those who were turned away, began setting up their own refugee camps as they tried to flee from the U.S. into Texas.

Pulling off the head phones Josh picked up the walkie talkie, "Robert, we need to stop and talk. I've been watching some stuff online and we've got a couple of problems to deal with."

"Okay, as soon as we spot a safe place we'll pull over."

Robert pulled into the parking lot of an old closed down convenience store and parked in the rear of the building out of sight from the road. The Jeep parked along side and all three slipped into the van.

"What's so important? We've only been on the road for an hour. We're not gonna make any time if we keep stopping," Robert said.

"Two things, we all need to know about. First, they have roadblocks up on every road leading into Texas. They won't let us in and since we've all been stripped of our U.S. Citizenship, they'll arrest us and put us into one of the detention camps."

"I figured we could probably sneak in on one of the small country roads," Robert said.

"The way it sounded, every road was guarded. If we're gonna get in we'll have to do it like the illegals used to before they opened the borders."

"Okay, that shouldn't be too hard. There's a lot of open country along the Louisiana and Texas border. What's the second thing we need to all know?"

"It appears that President Watson is taking over the U.S. With full martial law. The civil rights of those who have been protesting have been violated. There are riots happening all over the country."

"Well," said Joe. "That's what full martial law does. It suspends the Constitution. Allowing the military to set up curfews and relocate any one, to anywhere, it wants. It allows for confiscation of firearms and they can arrest whoever they decide might be a threat, real or perceived."

"They don't have many guns to worry about," stated Blaine. "Ever since the Obama administration's gun control act of 2013 very few citizens have any thing besides a shotgun and maybe a six shooter. All the automatic stuff was outlawed. Law abiding people had to give up their right to bear arms. Even us veterans had to give ours up. Even with all the perks I had, as a Medal of Honor recipient, I was forced to hand over all my registered weapons."

"Blaine, you've got a Medal of Honor," exclaimed Sally. "Only a handful of men got one of those and lived to tell about it. I'd love to hear your story."

"Maybe one of these days I'll share it. I can say I'd rather have my leg than the medal," he said slapping his prosthetic.

Robert broke into the conversation. "Looks like we're gonna have to be extra careful. Keep an eye out for the military. I assume that they'll be patrolling any hot spots. Josh will you be able to get a moment-by-moment scope of things online as we travel?"

"Yeah, it shouldn't be a problem. The downside is that I need to use my own cell, because the trac phones we got didn't come with a data package. There's a possibility, although slim, that they could track my number."

"That's a chance we'll have to take. We need to know what's going on in front of us. Keep it live and keep us informed. We need to get moving. Joe's gonna be driving for us and I'll try to map out a plan and location to get us into Texas. The rest of you, if you're not driving, get some shut eye."

"Blaine, Josh is gonna have to be online and I'm beat could you drive the Jeep?"

"Sure thing, Addi. You and that baby get some rest."

* * * * *

"Chief Fife, the phone company on line one." Susan said. "They have one of the numbers you gave to them, being used right now. They want to know what you want them to do with it."

"Great, we'll get the Laziers now."

"It's not their phone. This one belongs to Joshua Daniels and it's heading west so he's most likely not with Chief Lazier. Wasn't he headed southeast?" Susan asked.

"You should know the answer to that, you sent out the bolo."

"Phil told me they were going southeast so I

needed to alert the authorities from here to the East Coast. So that's what I did.

'

"What! Get Davis in here," Fife shouted. "He knew they were headed west to Texas."

"Okay, but you better pick up on line one."

"Hello, this is Chief Fife. What do you have for me?"

"Good afternoon, Chief. Joshua Daniel's cell is being used down by Sandy Springs, Georgia."

"How close can you pinpoint it?"

"I can give you the road and what direction it's moving."

"Go ahead tell me."

"It's on US-19 which is also known as the South Georgia 400. It looks like maybe 15 miles North of Sandy Springs."

"Thank you. Keep an eye on it as long as possible. If it changes direction or roads let me know right away."

"No problem Chief."

Hanging up he called in his office assistant. "Susan, get the State police located around the Sandy Springs, Georgia area, on the line."

"Yes sir, right away. Phil's on his way in. He was out in the foothills so it'll be about 20 minutes."

"Chief, the Georgia State police are on line

one."

"Hello, this is Police Chief Bernard Fife of Walhalla, South Carolina, who am I speaking with?"

"Chief Fife, this is Sergeant Petrie what can I do for you?"

"Sergeant, I have some fugitives out your way and I would like you to pick them up."

"Who and where are they?"

"They're being tracked via cell phone about 15 miles or so north of Sandy Springs. Their names are Robert and Sally Lazier and Josh and Addison Daniels. They are probably armed and considered dangerous."

"We'll do what we can, but the situation down here is not good. All of our men and women are tied up with crowd control and dispersing all the protesters. We have very few troopers free to patrol the roadways. If I were you I wouldn't expect anything from us. Do you have the license plate number and vehicle they are in?"

"They're driving a brown minivan, South Carolina plates WL-63812. They might also be in a blue Jeep Wrangler, plate number WL-63004."

"Chief, I'll put out a bolo for them but again don't expect much. We'll let you know if we find them."

"Chief, Phil is waiting to see you."

"Thanks Susan, send him in."

"Take a seat, Davis. Susan tells me you told her the Laziers were heading southeast and for her to put out a bolo to the East Coast. Is that true?" Fife asked angrily.

"Gosh, I don't think so," he said a bit taken back. "I suppose it is possible, it was early and I was still a little shook up."

"Shook up from what?" Fife asked. "nothing happened."

"I thought we were gonna be in a shoot out with Lazier. Man, I was scared to death. That guy's a crack shot and he's spent 20 plus years killing people in Iraq and Afghanistan. I didn't want to be next."

"Listen, if I find out that you tipped him off you'll find yourself behind bars."

"I'd never go against your orders Chief. I'm clean on this one."

Chapter Twenty-Four

"Follow 285 to the West," Josh said. We want to miss Atlanta, no telling what mess they've got."

"Yeah, I'd hate to get caught up in some protest. My goal is to fight for Texas to become free not spend my time in some detention camp"

"It's a shame we need to leave our own country to help Texas. We sure have come a long way in four years. What's your story with your leg and all?"

"I don't usually talk about it, because it ticks me off that I sacrificed so much for my country's freedom and they throw it all away. But I guess I can share it with you."

"Addi are you awake? Blaine's gonna tell us about his leg and Medal of Honor."

"Yeah, I'm just resting some but I really

want to hear."

"Okay, but no questions until I'm all done. Just let me talk and Josh, you keep an eye on your laptop."

"Yeah, no sweat."

"I was on my second deployment. We were stationed in the Helmand Province in South Afghanistan. My Special Forces unit was the only Army unit around. The U.S. contingent in the area were the 3rd Battalion, 4th Marines.

"We had just finished a mission and had arrived back at the main base when all hell broke lose. The area we were in was at the base of some small hills sorta like the foothills of South Carolina.

"Unfortunately, the Taliban had all kinds of places to hide. They had three different light artillery units set-up about 200 yards out and they began shelling the base. The Marines were able to take out two of the three with grenade launchers. The third was under cover and out of range.

"Being Special Forces I thought I was invincible. I took off toward the location with a grenade launcher. They kept shelling the compound and our boys were getting clobbered. Fortunately I had a lot of cover from the Marines and the landscape. When I got to where I could actually see the artillery I launched a grenade. I was about twenty yards to the left," he said motioning with his left hand.

"The Taliban lobbed a grenade my way and it took off my leg just below the knee. I was able to get another Grenade launched after that and took them out. At least that's what they told me, I don't remember a thing after I was hit. Later, while I was recovering form my wounds a bunch of Marines came by for a visit. They expressed how I had saved hundreds of lives that day. Their Colonel was putting me in for the Medal of Honor. That's about all there is to it."

"All there is to it,"exclaimed Addi patting him on the back. "You're a hero."

"You mentioned something about special privileges that came with the medal. What was that all about?" Josh asked.

"That was kind of cool. I received a little over a thousand dollars more each month as a recipient. I was getting full 100% disability and got that bonus on top of it. Of course once they found out I signed a petition for secession they took it all away from me and wanted me to pay it back.

"Medal of Honor recipients also get a bunch of other perks just because of their sacrifices. But they were quick to take it all away. That's why I get so mad when I see our government taking away

163

what I and so many others fought for."

"I, for one, appreciate knowing you. And I'm glad you're on my side."

I'll agree with that," said Addi.

* * * * *

Meanwhile, back in the minivan, Robert is searching for one of the trac phones. "I need to give Colonel Bowie a call to let him know we should be in Texas late Thursday night. Sally, have you seen one of the prepaid phones that Josh bought?"

"I think there in one of the back packs. I'll look through them," she said rummaging through the closest one. "Here's one. You know how to use it?"

"Woman, don't give me any of your smart mouth," he said with a grin.

She scooted to the front of her seat and grabbed him in a mock choke hold as she brought her face around to his cheek and planted a big kiss. "Just messin with ya honey."

He smiled as he turned on the phone and dialed Bowie's cell.

"This is Colonel Bowie. Who this?"

"Sir, it's Sergeant Major Lazier."

"Are you in Texas yet?"

"No sir. We should be crossing the border sometime tonight. I heard all the roads are blocked. Anything you can do about that?"

"I'm afraid not Sergeant Major. They have them set-up about a mile out from the actual border. Do you know where you want to cross?"

"Somewhere along I-20 a little southwest of Shreveport," he said, looking at the map on his lap.

"Okay. Take this number down and give Staff Sergeant Jones a call when you get close and need a diversion. I'll have him blow something up and cause a good ole Texas ruckus. You should be able to get across about a mile South."

"That sounds like a plan sir. How's President Bent's wife doing?"

"I haven't talked with him, but from what I understand she's holding her own. Thanks for asking. It's been hard on him. Say a prayer or two for them."

"I have sir, I have. Been saying a few for you as well. How's your militia holding up?"

"They're not doing to bad. Wish you were here to help them. Once you get across the border the staff sergeant will get you a straight flight to me. How many you got with you?"

"Two Army guys, one's a Medal of Honor recipient who lost his leg in Afghanistan. One computer expert, his pregnant wife and my Sally."

"Why don't you send the ladies to my place just outside of Austin. They'll be safer with my wife and they can unite together in their prayers for us. I'll give Staff Sergeant Jones the address and he'll take care of them. Can both the Special Forces guys still fight?"

"They'll both do fine. Sir, I'm looking forward to serving under your command again. I'll call when we get in the air."

"Good, I'll be glad to have you on staff again Lazier. Get here soon."

Robert hung up and grabbed his road atlas. Finding Shreveport, Louisiana he followed I-20 West with his finger. The last exit in Louisianan was about three miles from the border and he was sure the roadblock would be shortly after the exit. This would keep people from turning around when they saw the blockade. He decided they would take exit 5 onto US80 West and then take Elysian Fields Road South to the Crooked Hollow Golf Course. His plan had them leaving the minivan at the golf course parking lot and taking the Jeep across the rugged terrain to the border late on Thursday.

"Joe, when we get to Shreveport take the bypass and look for a rest stop. I need to share our plan for tonight."

Chapter Twenty-Five

"I haven't seen any signs of a rest area coming up anytime soon and we're running out of gas. I think I'll stop at exit 11 after we get back on US 20. We can meet there and you can fill everyone in on the plans for tonight."

"Yeah, that'll be fine, Joe. We could all use a short break and something to drink. I'll let Josh and them know," said Robert reaching for the walkie talkie. "How far is it?"

"Only about eight miles."

"Okay, but pull off to the side so we don't stand out."

After filling up, Joe parked the van on the West side of the building and Josh pulled alongside. They all got in the van and Robert laid out his plan for crossing the border. Once they all knew what to expect, Robert, Sally and Blaine went inside the convenience store to use the restroom. The rest began getting all their essentials moved from the van to the Jeep making sure there was room for all six to ride.

"Honey, a State trooper just walked in," Sally whispered as Robert walked out of the bathroom.

"Just play it cool. Don't get excited or nervous. We're just driving through stopping for a snack. He has no reason to talk to us," he told her as they walked up to the counter.

Blaine was two rows over looking at the soft drinks. Unaware that the policeman was walking up behind him, He opened the cooler door and bent down to grab a coke showing a glimpse of the revolver stuck in his waistband.

The Trooper stopped and reaching for his weapon he felt a gun barrel in the small of his back. "Not a smart move Trooper. Relax and no one will get hurt," said Robert taking the trooper's weapon out of the holster. "Blaine, get the clerk before he sets off an alarm. Hands behind your back please," he said reaching for the man's cuffs.

"What're we gonna do with them?" Blaine asked.

"Lock them in the back room, turn the closed sign on the window and lock the front door.

He probably just stopped for a drink. I'm sure no one is coming to look for him, for a while at least."

"What about his police car?" Sally asked.

"Baby, I knew I trained you right. We'll take it down the road a piece and park it along side the highway. That'll keep his department looking in the wrong place."

"Joe, follow me. I'm gonna take the cop car about five miles and park it along the road," Robert told him as he jumped in the front seat.

When he pulled off on the shoulder he noticed a sharp drop off and decided to put the cruiser in neutral and push it down into the ditch. *That ought to be hidden for a while.* Wiping the dirt off his hands he jumped in the van sliding door and they took off.

"Let's go. Get to exit 5 and we'll be in Texas in no time. Yee Ha, yippe ki a," said Robert waving an imaginary cowboy hat.

It wasn't long before they pulled into the Crooked Hollow Golf Course lot. Gathering the last of their weapons they piled into the Jeep as Robert made the call to Sergeant Jones.

"Staff Sergeant Jones, what can I do for you?"

"Hello Sergeant. This Sergeant Major Robert Lazier. Colonel Bowie told you about us."

169

"Yes sir. I have a diversion all set up just let me know when you want it and where you're crossing."

"We're down off Elysian Fields Road by the golf course. It's about three quarters of a mile to the border through the back country. Give us five minutes, then do what you've got planned."

"Yes sir. I'll have some men head down that way to pick you up. They'll have my phone so you can call them when you get on the friendly side."

"Okay guys, let's roll. All hell is gonna break lose in five."

Dodging trees and shrubs in the dark was not easy for Josh and the going was slow. It was obvious to all in the Jeep that he had driven off-road before as he inched his way toward Texas. Suddenly the sky lit up as mortars exploded three miles north. The noise and confusion left those in the area confused. Unfortunately, it also caused the military border patrol to look toward it.

""What's that coming from the South? Addi asked.

"Man, that's border patrol. You better get this thing movin or we won't make it without a fight," yelled Robert, pulling out his phone. "Sergeant Jones?"

"No sir this is Corporal Haddin."

"How close are you to us Corporal?"

"We'll blink our lights. Can you see them?"

"Yeah, do you have a grenade launcher with you?"

"Yes sir."

"Great, when we blink our lights, lob a couple grenades in front of the other vehicle. Try to slow them down."

"Will do sir."

"Head for those lights across the border Josh. We're almost there," he said as a grenade went off 20 yards behind them.

"I see a fence about 200 yards out," shouted Blaine. "That's gotta be Texas. Drive right over it and don't stop."

Once the fence was torn down the Texas men opened fire on the border patrol and they stopped the chase. The Jeep and Humvee drove about a quarter mile into Texas before they stopped to make sure everyone was okay.

"Corporal, I'm Sergeant Major Lazier. This here's my wife, Sally."

"Nice to meet you ma'am."

"The driver is Josh and his wife, Addi."

The corporal tipped his helmet and said. "Good driving, son."

"These two are our Army guys, Blaine and

171

Joe."

"Glad to meet you both," said the corporal shaking hands. "Staff Sergeant Jones, has everything ready for you at the base camp. We should get up there, Sergeant Major."

"By all means. Lead the way soldier."

* * * * *

The US 20 base camp, consisted of about 200 soldiers from the Texas National Guard, led by Staff Sergeant Scott Jones. Their main task was to keep the border secure. They had a dozen or so Hummer's and Jeeps that they used to travel up and down the fence line. They manned the road blocks on all the major roads and a few of the lesser traveled roads.

"Sergeant Jones, it's good to meet you. Good job on the diversion. Your Corporal did well."

"You're a legend, Sergeant Major Lazier, it's my honor. I have some rooms set aside for you and your men at the motel two miles up the road. You can get a decent night's sleep before we send the ladies to Austin."

"When can the rest of us get up to Colonel Bowie."

"We'll have a small plane fly you up first

thing in the morning."

"Sounds good, Staff Sergeant. Fill me in on what's happening as far as the protection of the border."

"I'm only an enlisted man so I don't know much."

"Bowie put you in charge of over two hundred men. He doesn't do that unless he has a lot of trust in your ability to lead and he doesn't let an individual lead without telling them what they need to know. So, Staff Sergeant, tell me what he told you."

"Yes sir. There are fifty units like this one spread out along the Louisianan and Oklahoma borders. We're not expecting much from those directions because both States are friendly and are resisting the Feds the best they can.

"We have a larger contingency along the smaller Arkansas border but really don't expect much there. Along the Mexican-Texas border the Mounted Border Patrol, continues to police that area. They're an elite group and no one'll get past em. I understand they've also branched up along the southern part of the New Mexico line. The majority of the Militia has been moved to the northern two-thirds of the western border. That's where Colonel Bowie's headquarters are located. He's got just under eight hundred men against the 3rd Battalion, 7th Marines and I heard there's another Battalion coming."

"I was afraid it would be the 3 / 7. I served under Colonel Bowie when he commanded them. I know most of the corporals and sergeants in that outfit. Good men and excellent warriors. They'll be a tough fight."

"Yes sir, Sergeant Major. Let's get your team to the motel we leave at 0700."

* * * * *

"Robert, I don't like the idea of being separated from you," said Sally sitting cross legged on the bed.

"You know I can't take you to the front lines. You and Addi will be safer in Austin with Mrs. Bowie."

"I know, but that doesn't mean I like the idea. Malinda is nice and we get along great and I'm looking forward to seeing her again but I'm afraid for you."

"Baby, we've been through this before. I'll do my best to be smart and safe."

"This isn't like your other deployments. You're gonna be fighting some of your closest

174

friends and I know about your soft spots. You and I both know you're not as tough as you make yourself out to be."

"That's a concern for me as well. But the freedom of our country demands that I do this. I've fought all my life for our freedom, I can't stop now. I'll try to talk with Klink and see if he'll spread the word that I'm fighting for freedom. Who knows, it might cause some of the Marines to jump ship."

"Enough talk about fighting. Come to bed this may be our last night together for quite some time," she said holding out her arms for him.

* * * * *

At 0645, Robert, pulled Sally into his arms for one last kiss. They were standing on the passenger side of the Black SUV. Josh and Addi were on the driver's side, saying the same goodbye, see you shortly, I'll be okay speech. The car pulled away with both their faces looking back through the rear window with an "I don't expect to see you again" look. Josh with his hand raised with a slight movement and Robert throwing a kiss to the love of his life. As they pulled out of sight, headed for Austin, Josh walked over to Robert and asked. "Do you think we'll ever see them again?"

"Josh, I've been on seven deployments to intense battle sights. I always planned on coming home to my wife. That's my plan for this deployment. Keep your focus on what needs to be done and the love of your wife in your heart, counting the days until you can hold her in your arms again. Believe, that you will make love to her in the near future," he said slapping Josh on the back. "Come on, son, we need to get up North."

"Thank you, Robert . . . er, maybe I should start calling you Sarge," he said as they walked toward to the small twin engine plane sitting on the grassy runway.

"That would be Sergeant Major to you, son," he said with deep guttural voice. "I like you and all but you're right, military respect is important as we go into battle. When we meet up with Colonel Bowie, I'll see if I can't get you in the ranks as a corporal. I think you've got what it takes to lead."

"I've never been in the military sarge – I mean Sergeant Major." How high up is a corporal?"

"Well rest assured we won't put you on the front lines. I know you're good with the computer so we'll see if we can't get you cracking some of their codes."

"You didn't answer my question. How high up is a corporal?"

"I don't know when it comes to the Texas militia, but in the Marine Corp a corporal is over 80 percent of the enlisted men," said Robert as they boarded the plane.

The twin Cessna Turbo airplane held six people including the pilot. Robert noticed the well worn interior with torn carpet and ratty looking seats. The headliner was drooping and the windows were clouded over. He looked over at Joe and raised his eyebrows. Joe gave an, oh no look back.

"What year is this plane?" asked Blaine as all four of the passengers turned an ear to hear what the aged pilot had to say.

"This beauty is a 1963 Skyknight 320 turbo prop Cessna. I've owned it since the day it came off the showroom floor. It was the cream of the crop then and as far as I'm concerned still is."

"1963! My dad wasn't even born when this thing was made," said a startle Josh. "Is it gonna make it off the runway?"

"You just never mind, sonny. I've kept it in tip top condition. Why I had it completely rebuilt after the crash," the old timer said with a smirk.

"Crash! I survived Afghanistan, I don't want to go down in some Texas wilderness,"exclaimed Blaine.

"I wasn't talking about a plane crash," he

said. "I meant the crash of the housing market a few years ago. Man, you young'ens are easy."

The plane bounced and rocked as it went down the grassy runway before lifting up and barely clearing the top of the trees. Robert got a kick out of Josh's pale face and white knuckles as he held on for dear life.

"How long's the flight gonna be?" Robert asked.

"Depending on how much wind we hit I'm thinkin about an hour and a half or so."

* * * * *

The old timer was right. Thought Robert as he looked at his watch. *Exactly an hour and a half.* Looking out the widow as they taxied up to the terminal he saw a good collection of fighter jets with huge yellow roses painted on the tails. Two were in the process of taking off from the same runway they had just landed on. *At least we have some air support. They'll come in handy.*

"Here we are gentlemen. Hope you enjoyed your flight and please remember to fly Ancient Air next time you travel."

"Thanks old man. You got us here safely. I wasn't sure if you or the plane would live long enough," Josh said, patting the pilot on the

178

shoulder.

"You keep yourself out of harms way sonny. Good luck."

"Why does everyone call me sonny or son. I'm 23 years old," mumbled Josh as he departed the old plane.

"What did you say?" Robert asked.

"Just talking to myself, Sergeant Major."

"Okay, son," he said smiling.

Chapter Twenty-Six

Delores and four of President Bent's staff, were busy setting up the make shift office at the Beaumont Inn. The three upstairs bedrooms had been hastily cleared of the furnishings. New desks chairs, phone lines and computer system were installed. Lieutenant Tucker added six more Texas Rangers for security. Mrs Herbert made sure the fourth bedroom was in order for President Bent when he returned from the hospital.

"Mrs. Herbert, I am sorry to put you and your bed and breakfast through all of this."

"Mr. President, I am at your beck and call. Whatever you need, we will get for you. How is your lovely wife doing?" She asked reaching out for his arm.

"She's still in guarded condition. The doctors think she will make it but will need a lot of therapy. Thank you for asking."

"Is there any thing I can get for you?"

"If you don't mind, I would like a hot cup of black coffee. I think I'm gonna have a long night in front of me."

"I'll brew a fresh pot and bring it up," she said with a consoling smile.

"Do you have any pie or desert?"

"Yes sir, I'll fix you right up," she said as she headed down the stairs to the kitchen.

"Delores," said the President. "Are the phones ready?"

"Yes sir, Mr. President. Who would you like to call?"

"James Bowie. I'll be in my office when you get him on the line. Lieutenant Tucker, when Mrs. Herbert comes up, with the coffee,will you join me. I'd like to talk over what happened earlier."

"Yes sir."

* * * * *

Mrs. Herbert was making the coffee and setting some freshly made pound cake out when her husband, Carl entered. "Honey, isn't it exciting to have the President and his people here with us?" She asked turning to look at him.

"I don't know Dot. What if Texas loses and we're branded traitors because we let him stay at our place?"

"Hush your mouth, somebody might hear you," she loudly whispered.

"I could care less. Look, I'm in favor of seceding. I don't like the way things have been going any more than the next guy. But I also don't want to spend my golden years in some God forsaken detention camp. Or worse, get put in front of a firing squad as a traitor during war time."

"Oh come on. That'll never happen."

"Did you think they would ambush Bent? Four Texas Rangers were murdered."

"You do have a point."

"You bet I do, sweetie. On the other hand if we win, the bed and breakfast will go hog wild. We won't be able to keep people away. The publicity we will get because the president made it his home away from home while his wife lay in the hospital, within an inch of her life, is priceless."

"Well, you figure out how we can add on," she said smiling. "I've gotta get this coffee and cake up to our guest of honor," she said giving him a peck on the cheek.

Traversing the stairs she reached the President's new office where Lieutenant Tucker was waiting.

"I'll take that Mrs. Herbert. Thank you very much."

"You're welcome," she said handing him the tray. "Have a good evening, Lieutenant."

"Same to you and Carl. Tell him we will win this battle for sovereignty. He won't spend a day in some God forsaken detention camp."

"Oh my goodness," she said putting her hand over her mouth. "You heard us? I'm so sorry."

"That's okay, we're all a little fearful about the whole thing. We just didn't have any other recourse."

"I know, Lieutenant. Carl, really is for the Republic of Texas. We're just scared. Our social security comes from the Federal government. We're afraid we'll lose everything."

"That's a major concern of the President. I think he has it all under control. Texas has had a strong economy and we're in the black. So, even though, you may suffer for a short time he has a plan in place to meet your needs once this battle is won."

Resting her hand on his arm she said. "Thank you so much for those encouraging words. They mean a lot to me."

Opening the door Tucker walked in the

office. President Bent was standing staring out the window overlooking the lights of Beaumont. His hands woven together at the small of his back. "Mr. President, your coffee and cake are here."

Wiping a tear from the side of his cheek he turned and walked to his desk. "Thank you Lieutenant," he said sitting in his chair. "Have a seat and join me. Mrs. Herbert gave us an extra cup and fork. She makes a killer pound cake."

"Don't mind if I do. I haven't eaten much since the ambush. What was it you wanted to talk about?"

"I need your expert opinion."

"On what, sir?"

"Do you think the ambush was pulled off by a rogue army unit or did Watson order it?"

"I'm in law enforcement, not the military, but in my honest opinion, and that's all it is, I think Watson ordered it. This was a Special Forces operation and I know the members of this elite fighting force are headstrong, but they're not foolish. They would never do something like this without orders," he said shaking his head.

"I agree with you. I'm just not sure how to handle the aftermath. Should I retaliate and try to take him out or should I back off and hope the rest of the country gets so enraged that they put a stop to him. If I had him in this room, I'd probably kill him. That frustrates me, because that isn't who I am. He's driving me nuts."

"Sir, that's understandable. He had you and your wife shot. Four Texas Rangers are dead and he deserves to die," he said leaning closer to the desk to make his point. "However, you cannot let him control who you are. You cannot stoop to his level."

"Thank you, Lieutenant. You have a level head and I appreciate that. Let's have some coffee and cake."

"Mr. President, Colonel Bowie is on line one."

"Thanks Delores," he said pushing the intercom and picking up the phone receiver. "Hello James," he said swallowing his cake. "Things have escalated."

"Yes they have, Mr. President."

Lieutenant Tucker started to get up to leave but the President waved for him to stay and enjoy his cake. He sat back down and grabbed a piece along with a cup of coffee.

Chapter Twenty-Seven

"Mr. President, how's Alyssa doing?"

"She's holding her own James. Doctors say the danger of infection is high because of where her injuries are located and toxins that escaped from her colon. But aside from that she should heal good as new. She'll need a colostomy bag for a couple of months but once the colon heals she'll be fine. Thanks for asking."

"That's great to hear. What can I do for you sir?"

"James, this ambush takes us to the next level. We need to be on red alert. If they'll ambush us coming back from a peace talk, there's no telling what's next. Is our air force ready to protect our air space?"

"I talked with General Snead yesterday and they are a go. Anything we need, he's confident they can supply it. It looks like we can handle any dog fight in the air but I'm worried about short range rockets. They have a range close to 100 miles and even though we have some old Iron Domes set up along the New Mexico border it still leaves a lot of other areas unprotected."

The Iron Dome was designed and used by Israel beginning in 2007 when the Hamas began sending daily rockets from Gaza. It became the most effective defense solution Israel had against short range rocket attacks. It was a sad day, on January 10, 2015, when the U.S. officially withdrew it's support for Israel. They fell to the Iranian siege only five months later. Over two million, Jewish Israeli citizens, were killed in the short Iran, Israel war.

"Those Iron Domes the ones that were left abandoned at Lackland?"

"Yes sir. I had them relocated, shortly after we first met in your office, in November. We're limited on ammunition for them but they will help out a lot in the beginning."

"Sounds like you have things under control Colonel. I'll touch base with you around ten tomorrow morning. Good night James."

"Good night Mr. President."

Bent grabbed the rest of his cake and topped

off his coffee. "Man, she makes a good pound cake."

"I'll agree with you on that," Tucker said. "How are things with the Colonel?"

"He seems to think we're all set. He's in agreement with us and hoping for no loss of life tomorrow. It's gonna be a long day. You should get some sleep."

"What about you Mr. President? You've been through a lot today, a good rest would help you and the Republic of Texas," Lieutenant Tucker said rising from his chair.

"I'll try to get some rest on the sofa over there," he said with a motion of his head.

"Mr. President, Governor Rickert is on line one."

"Thank You Delores," he said picking up the phone and motioning for Tucker to leave. "Hello Gene, what can I do for you?"

"Hal, how's Alyssa?"

"She's holding her own. Thanks for asking."

"I am sorry this took place in my State. I had no idea..."

"I never suspected you did Gene."

"Listen, the State of Louisiana has informed President Watson that we will not allow this battle to include our boundaries. We've been forced to allow blockades on all the roads but that is the limit. Anything else will not be allowed. We are behind you all the way. Governor Hashley, from Oklahoma, has told me the same thing."

"Thank you, Gene, and if you talk with John thank him for me as well. You do realize that under Martial Law you won't have a choice."

"We understand that but we're hoping President Watson won't want more discord than he already has."

"I hope so. Tomorrows gonna be a huge day for us. If we can hold the initial attack from crossing the border we may have a chance."

"The world will be watching and most will be on your side. Sorry, I called so late. Get some rest. Goodbye."

Well it seems everyone wants me to get some rest. I suppose I should at least lay down. Walking over to the sofa and sitting on the edge he called out to the Lord in a brief prayer.

"Lord, be with Alyssa. Help her to heal quickly and give the kids traveling safety as they come to be with her tomorrow.

"Father, I know that You are still in control, that You care of us and that You never ever make a mistake. But for some reason it's hard to make sense of all that has taken place in the U.S. I know when we removed out support from Your chosen people, Israel, we were in trouble. I guess what has taken place the past few years should not surprise anyone who spends time in Your Word.

"Lord help us tomorrow. Work it out so that no more lives are lost. And Lord, help me to forgive Nicholas Watson for what he did to Alyssa, the Texas Rangers and their families. At the same time Lord, take him out of the picture, however, You see fit.

In Jesus' name amen."

Stretching out on the sofa he added to his prayer, "Lord help my mind slow down so I can sleep."

Chapter Twenty-Eight

President Bent woke to the noise of Lieutenant Tucker setting up a television set in the corner of the room.

"Mr. President, you need to see this. There has been breaking news concerning the ambush. Apparently, one of the men involved has defected to Texas and is spilling his guts."

"Really. What's he have to say?" The President asked sitting up and stretching his shoulders.

"You need see it first hand. The conservative networks are playing it non-stop. Can't find anything on the big three stations."

"Well, we all know that's normal," said Bent as he sat up with his eyes intently on the T.V. set. "They never did report the truth. They've always been way left of the regular guy on the street."

"Here's the story," Tucker said taking a seat.

"For those just joining our broadcast let me replay what Corporal Jason Hatch, one of the Army Special Forces members, involved in the recent ambush of Halford Bent and his security team, has stated in an interview with Brian James on Fox and Friends."

"Corporal Hatch, you are claiming to have been involved in the ambush of the Republic of Texas President and his security forces. What can you tell us about the ambush?"

"First, let me say I am not proud of what took place. I hope the president's wife pulls through. I am sorry about the murder of the Texas Rangers and my heart goes out to their families. If I could change things I would."

"What was your part in the ambush?"

"I was the driver of the Humvee involved in the chase. You need to understand I was just following orders," he said brushing a tear from his eye. "I did what my superiors told me to do. That's how I was trained."

"That's how the military works," Brian said. "Who gave the orders to take out President Bent?"

"The orders came directly from President Watson. Our 1st Lieutenant received the call and the plan was put into motion."

"How did you know it was directly from President Watson?

"When Lieutenant Alfonso hung up he said our Commander in Chief gave the go ahead. It was very obvious who made the call. We were all sworn to secrecy."

"Why are you coming forward?" Brian asked.

"Because, I signed up to defend the liberty and freedom of our country, not to kill innocent men and women. President Watson has overstepped his authority. When I heard him flat out lie on National T.V. I knew I was on the wrong side of this war."

"What do you think should happen to you?"

"I assume that I will stand trial for my part of the ambush. Although, I'm not sure the Texan's will let me live very long. They are pretty ticked off."

"Corporal Hatch, you were simply following orders in a time of war, don't you think that should come under consideration?"

"No, I don't. I would consider my actions a war crime and I deserve to pay for it."

"There you have it folks. The ambush on President Bent, his wife and security team was ordered by, none other than, the President of the

United States of America."

"I had no doubt it was Watson who ordered the action on us. Where's Corporal Hatch now?" Bent asked.

"He is under arrest just South of here in Port Arthur."

"Get him up here, I want to talk with him face to face."

"Sir, are you sure of that?"

"Yes, Lieutenant, I am."

"I'll take care of that right away. You need to listen to more of this news cast and if you can, get in touch with some of the folks you know in Washington. People are pretty ticked off at Watson right now. You may be able to slow down or get rid of the order to attack."

"Thanks Lieutenant. Would you ask Delores to please get me a small breakfast up here."

President Bent continued to watch the news, soaking in the different individuals asking and demanding that U.S. President Watson answer for what happened. *The lieutenant is right I do need to call some of the people I know in D.C.* Then speaking out load he said, "What time is it?" as he walked over and looked at his desk clock. "Seven. That gives me six hours to demand some extra time."

"What was that Mr. President?" Delores asked as she entered with his breakfast.

"Good morning Delores. I was just talking to myself. What did Mrs. Herbert send up?"

"Just a couple of eggs, bacon and toast," she said pouring him a cup of coffee.

"Thank her for me. I need you to get Senators Brown and Brennen on the phone for me before you do anything else."

"Yes sir, right away,"she said walking out the door.

Taking a sip of his coffee and small bite of toast his mind wandered to Alyssa. He had not heard anything from the hospital and was sure that she was doing okay. Hoping that she understood the dire straights he was in with the threat of an attack looming over them. He prayed that she was still in the induced coma and that when she woke it would all be behind them. That the Republic of Texas would be free and not a pile of rubble.

"Mr. President, Senator Brennen is on line one and Senator Brown is unavailable."

"Thank you. Give Congressman Doyle a try," he said picking up line one. "Hello Darren."

"Hal, how you holding up? How's Alyssa?"

"She's still in guarded condition in an induced coma. The doctors seem to think she'll come out of it okay if she can fend off any infections. Thanks for asking."

"That's good, but how are you doing? You have a lot on your plate."

"That's why I called Darren. I'm sure you heard the news about who ordered the ambush."

"Yes. I can hardly believe it."

"What do you think you can do to stop this madman from attacking Texas?"

"Hal, I realize he didn't do right by you and your family. But be careful about calling him a madman. He is still the President of the United States."

"You're right, I'm just so concerned about Alyssa and the families of the four Rangers that were murdered. I'm not thinking straight or acting like I belong to the Lord. I'm sorry."

"No need to apologize to me. I just don't want you to say it to the wrong person. You've got enough to deal with as it is."

"Darren, can you rally some of the Senators to force Watson to at least postpone the attack?"

"I figured that's why you called. I not only will but have already begun to do it. I've gotten a lot of support. Folks are not happy with the way the President is taking the bull by the horns. I'll continue to get a contingent together and insist on a meeting with him."

"Thanks Darren, I knew I could count on you. You've been a good friend for years."

"I'll let you know what he says as soon as possible," Senator Brennen said hanging u the phone.

"Mr. President, Congressman Doyle, on line two."

"Thank you," he said switching over to line two. "Hello Congressman Doyle."

"Hello Governor Bent. What can I do for you?"

"Congressman," he said ignoring that he called him Governor. "I'm sure you've heard that President Watson ordered the attack on my security force yesterday."

"Yes I did and I'm sorry for the loss of your men and the wounding of your wife. But what do you want me to do about it?"

"I was hoping, I could get you to contact some of the other members of congress and ask President Watson to hold off on attacking Texas."

"I can certainly try but we are under full martial law and he is the Commander in Chief."

"Does that give him the right to do whatever he wants to do. Isn't there some control the legislature has?" Bent asked in a slight huff.

"There's supposed to be, but it appears that Watson doesn't agree with that and feels he has every right to fight for keeping our United States United."

"Congressman, you know, as well as I do, that he is dividing this country not uniting it."

"I'll do what I can but no guarantees."

"Thank you, Congressman. I'm sure you know that time is short."

"Yes I do. I'll get on the phone right away."

"Okay, goodbye," he said hanging up.

Finishing his breakfast of now cold eggs and coffee, the President washed up and put on a change of clothes. Sitting down he opened his Bible and read out loud from Proverbs 3:5-6. *"Trust in the LORD with all your heart, And lean not on your own understanding; In all your ways acknowledge Him, and He shall direct your paths. Do not be wise in your own eyes; Fear the LORD and depart from evil. It will be health to your flesh, and strength to your bones."*

"Lord help me to do this today and every day."

Chapter Twenty-Nine

Senator Brennen began calling his fellow senators. At nine o'clock he had been able to reach sixty-two of the remaining ninety-seven. Twelve of those, all Democrats, were in the President's corner and expected him to take full control of the military and put down this nonsensical rebellion. Five Republicans and two Democrats, had decided to stay neutral and not lend their support for fear of future reprisals. The remaining 43 bi-partisan men and women were dead set against taking military action against Texas at this time. They were appalled, President Watson ordered the ambush and had denied it.

Brennen's final call was to Vice President Angelica Chandler who resides over the Senate. "Madam, Vice President, I have gathered 44 Senators, including myself. We don't want to see any military action taken against Texas until we can get to the bottom of the ambush."

"Senator, you know we ran our campaign with world peace as our main platform, I personally agree with you."

"Thank you Ma'am."

"Let me finish Senator," she said impatiently. "Although, I agree personally, I am under obligation to follow my President's leading. I may not like what he is doing but I have to stand behind him as the leader of this great country."

"Look Angelica, let's be candid. Watson is going to destroy this country from within if he continues to push his power past what it is."

"Darren, all I can do is attempt to set up a meeting between the two of you. I'm not in a position where I want to cross the man."

"Okay Madam Vice President, I'll accept that. It needs to be this morning."

"I'll try to set it up. My assistant will get back with you. Goodbye Senator, and good luck."

"Thank you, Ma'am"

* * * * *

Congressman John Doyle decided to use the computer to rally his peers. He wrote a brief email and sent it to all of the 435 members of the House.

Dear Fellow Congressman,

It is with deep regret that I send this communication. The last week has been an extremely difficult one for our country. With the demand of Texas for secession, many folks, from shore to shore, are having their citizenship revoked. The recent ambush, on Halford Bent and his security force, have only added to the confusion.

Although, I am 100% against giving in to Texas' demand, I am also 100% against using military force until we have had ample opportunity for a peaceable solution.

Since being under full martial law has apparently given all control over to President Watson, the checks and balances of our country have been eliminated. I am in the process of setting up a meeting with the President in order to ask him to reconsider using military force at one this afternoon.

It would be beneficial, if I had the support of the majority of the House. Because time is short, I have set up a brand new email account. Please respond within one hour to against@govmail.com only if you are against using military force at this time. I will count the number and use it in my meeting with the President.

Thank you.

Congressman John Doyle

"Sally, call the White House and see if I can get an immediate appointment with President Watson," he said to his administrative assistant.

"Yes sir, right away."

"Make sure it's before noon and keep trying no matter what."

Picking up his cell, Congressman Doyle, searched through his contact list until he found Senator Brennen's private number. "Good morning Senator, this is Congressman Doyle. Could you please give me a call back as soon as you get this voice mail. It is urgent that I talk with you this morning. Halford Bent said he asked you to talk with President Watson. He has asked me the same as House minority leader. I thought it would be nice if we could compare . . .beep"

* * * * *

"Hello, could I speak with Senator Brennen please."

"May I ask who's calling?" Asked the Senator's aid.

"Bill, Vice President Chandler's assistant."

"I'll connect you," she said as she buzzed the Senator. "The vice President's assistant Bill is on line one."

"Thank you, I've got it."

"Hello."

"Hello, Senator Brennen. The President will do a conference call with you and Congressman Doyle at precisely eleven-thirty. I'll call and set it up with your secretaries four or five minutes before then."

"Bill, I would rather have a face to face, if at all possible."

"Not going to happen today. He has a press conference at twelve-thirty and needs the time to prepare for it. Phone conference will have to do and you're lucky to get that Senator."

"I'll take what I can get. Thank you."

Picking up his cell he returned the congressman's call. "Congressman Doyle, this is Darren Brennen, how can I help you?"

"Hello Senator, my first name is John, okay if I call you Darren?"

"No problem, John."

Great, I just wanted to touch base with you. As I said in the voice mail, Halford Bent asked if I would talk with President Watson and said he had asked you to do the same. Since then, I received a call that we are to have a conference call with him at eleven-thirty and I just want to see if we're on the same page."

"Well John, there are forty four senators asking him to postpone the attack on Texas and I'm the spokes person."

"I have just about two hundred and twenty house members who want the same thing. I'm sure there are more but they haven't answered my email for whatever reason. I've gotta tell you, Darren, that I'm against the secession of Texas and will do whatever is necessary to keep them in the Union. I just want to give it a good peaceable try before we begin a civil war."

"John, it looks like we're on the same page. The key will be getting Watson to hold off. I don't expect him to do that but we've gotta try."

"Sounds good Senator. We'll talk at eleven-thirty. Goodbye."

Chapter Thirty

Eleven twenty-five, found both Senator Brennen and Congressman Doyle, nervously pacing the floor of their respective offices. At exactly eleven twenty-nine the secretaries buzzed them for their call.

"President Watson will be on in one minute. Your call will be limited to ten minutes," said the President's aid.

"Thank you," both men responded simultaneously.

"Senator Brennen and Congressman Doyle, it's good to hear from you both. How can I help you this morning?"

"Good morning, Mr. President, This is Senator Brennen. A large group of the Senators would like you to postpone the military attack on Texas."

"Sorry senator that's not going to happen."

"Mr. President, Congressman Doyle here. The majority of the house would concur with the Senate. Please hold off for a few days at least so we can . . . "

"Not gonna happen gentlemen," he said rudely. "My mind is made up. I will not allow the break up of the United States America under any circumstances. This is no difference than when Lincoln refused to allow the Southern states to split off."

"But sir, the Civil War was devastating. We don't need another one," Brennen said.

"Sir give us a few days to find a peaceable solution," Doyle piped in.

"I am sorry men but the only peaceable solution is for Texas to surrender before one this afternoon. So unless you have something else to say, I've got a press conference to get ready for."

"Sir, the majority of the legislature is against this attack and . . . "

"I'm in control until I lift martial law, if I ever lift it. Good day gentlemen."

The Senator looked at his receiver and mumbled something unmentionable, as the Congressman dialed the Senator's cell.

"Darren, this guys out for blood. He is mad

and I don't mean angry!"

"I warned Governor Bent about calling him a madman this morning, John. But he is out of control. We need to have a joint meeting with House and Senate as soon as we can. Let's set up a meeting in the House of Representative this afternoon."

"By then the invasion will be over," Doyle said in disbelief.

"I know. There's no way we can get everyone together any sooner. We've got to put our heads together and stop this from becoming an all out war between the States."

"Okay, let's shoot for three this afternoon in the house. We'll see you all there. Goodbye and good luck."

* * * * *

"Mr. President, you have thirty minutes before the conference," said Jim Simmens sticking his head into the room.

Jim was the President's right hand man. His job was to keep him on schedule, set-up appointments and do whatever was needed so that the President looked good. Jim loved his job but hated his boss. Although, Jim kept his politics out of his relationship with the President and his staff, he was a closet ultra conservative. He was good at what he did and blended into a room without notice.

"Thank you, Jim, and thanks for suggesting the Lincoln Memorial for this press conference. It is very fitting, considering we'll be entering the next Civil War in half an hour."

"You're welcome, sir. Perhaps they'll put a statue of you next to Lincoln."

"That's a nice thought. It's amazing how much we think alike."

"Thank you, Mr. President. Do you have all your notes?"

"I gave them to the media people. They'll get them on the teleprompter."

"You should take a hard copy just in case. We need to leave in five minutes to get there in plenty of time. The cars are waiting for us.

"It's a little chilly out there, so grab your overcoat, sir. I've gotta run to my office and grab mine. I'll meet you at the car," Jim said as he reached into his coat pocket for his private cell. As his office door closed behind him he asked, "Is everything ready?"

"We're all set on this end. Just make sure he's there."

* * * * *

Cameras and reporters from around the world were waiting on the steps of the Lincoln Memorial when the bullet proof cars pulled up. Secret service personnel, with white earphone wires protruding down their necks, had infiltrated the crowd. Agents surrounded the President's vehicle as they opened the doors and escorted him up the steps and into the memorial. The Secret Service was being extra cautious since this was a hastily prepared location. They had not had the opportunity to clear the entire area.

In four minutes, President Watson would give one last chance for Texas to back down from their demands. Standing in front of President Abraham Lincoln's statue he read, out load, the inscription above the larger than life Lincoln. "In this temple, as in the hearts of the people for whom he saved the Union, the memory of Abraham Lincoln is enshrined forever."

"Jim, who knows, the same could be my epitaph one day."

"That's certainly a possibility, Mr. President," he said as he looked off in the distance toward the WW II Memorial. "It's time, Mr. President. You're being introduced," Jim placed his hand on Watson's back and directed him toward the platform set up for him on the steps of the memorial.

"Ladies and gentlemen, the President of the United State of America."

Coming out from behind a large column, arms extended in a greeting he said. "Good afternoon. I am here today to issue one last warning to Texas Governor Halford Bent. Please rescind your demand for secession or we will be forced to use military strength to defend the Constitution of the United States.

"I am making this public announcement to assure every Texan that we do not want a fight. We want a peaceable solution to this situation. Give up your bid for independence and reunite with us.

"I did not have anything to do with the ambush of Governor Bent and his wife. The things being spread on the Internet are out and out lies. I did not order an assassination attempt of Bent's life and I do not want to invade Texas. However, I will not let even one State out of the Union.

"I'm delivering this message from the Lincoln Memorial because of what one of our greatest President's went through. We do not want a civil war. I do not want to make the same orders that Lincoln did. Please, Governor Bent, rescind your demand.

"At twelve forty-five I will call Governor Bent one last time for his decision. If he says no to my request, we will invade Texas with every ounce of our military force. We will not sto. . ."

The bullet caught the President's left ear and continued into the memorial disintegrating Lincoln's left knee. Secret service agents were all over the President whisking him inside the monument and out of site. Reporters and camera men were scurrying for cover while at the same time trying to record what was happening.

Washington Park Policemen quickly surrounded the building refusing anyone cover inside. Guns drawn waiting for whatever was next.

Running to the President's side Jim yelled, "We need to get him to a hospital right away," as he knelt down.

"I think I'm okay. The bullet just grazed my ear," he said reaching up and feeling where he had been hit. "Just get me to the car and out of here. We can stop the bleeding on the way to the White House. I still have a war that's gonna happen in twenty minutes."

"Okay men, form a shield and get Eagle to the car."

Six secret service agents quickly made a wedge in front of the President and made their way down the steps as the Park Police made a larger v-shape shield toward the car. In less than two minutes after Lincoln's knee cap was blasted, President Watson, was on his way to the Oval Office.

Three minutes earlier . . .

A large moving van came to an abrupt stop in front of the National World War II Memorial. The driver got out and quickly walked away from the truck toward the war memorial. Concealed behind the walls of the truck was a raised seat on top of a tripod. The person on the seat quickly and quietly opened a small sliding door near the top edge. Sliding the high-powered rifle into the mount she looked through the scope and took aim. Slowly squeezing the trigger she exhaled and at that very moment. . .

"Get this truck outta here," said a man banging on its side.

"Sh. . " said the shooter startled as the gun went off. She dropped down to the floor and quickly opened a side door and moved toward the driver who had shed his outer jacket and cap into a waste container. Slipping behind a small column she shock her hair out full length dropping her hat onto the ground. The couple grasped hands and scurried over to an information booth.

"What was that load noise? It sounded like a gun," exclaimed the woman to the lady behind the counter.

"I'm not sure what's going on. Stay here until we know for sure. The Park Police are pretty good about letting us know if there's any danger."

"Not a problem. We're just visiting from Georgia and don't want any trouble. We've heard bad things about D.C. at night. But this is broad daylight," said the driver. "Wow! Look at all the cop cars. I wonder what happened."

"I'll go ask one of the policemen," the information lady said.

"I jerked when that guy banged on the truck. I think I missed," whispered the shooter.

"Too bad," said the driver pulling her close as if comforting her. "Come on dear, everything will be okay," he said patting her back as the lady and a Park Policeman walked up. "Is everything okay?"

"Can I see some ID, please?"

"Yes sir. Honey, do you have your drivers license for the policeman?" He asked reaching in for his wallet. "Here's mine."

"Here you go officer," she said handing him her license.

"From Georgia, huh. You folks been at the war memorial very long?"

"No we just walked in when we heard a load shot. Or at least I think it was a shot."

"Did you see anything out of the ordinary?"

"No sir, did you see anything baby?" He asked as she shook her head. "What happened?"

"Someone took a shot at the President."

"Oh no," she gasped covering her mouth with her hand. "Is he alright?"

"Yes, he was only grazed. We're gonna have to hold you for a while."

"Why, we haven't done anything," he exclaimed.

"Well Mr. Black," said the officer glancing down at his license. "We need to check you both out before we can let you go. This is pretty serious and we'll be searching everybody we find. I hope you understand the situation we find ourselves in."

"Yes of course, Officer. Whatever we can do."

"Where's your car parked? We'll have to search it."

"We took public transit in. Our car is still at the motel, in Falls Church."

"Smart move. Beats having to find a parking place in the District. Let's go over to my cruiser and you can sit there while we run a background check."

Sitting in the back of the squad car the Blacks watch as a team of secret service agents comb through the moving van. Policemen and military personnel were searching the entire area, between the Lincoln Memorial and the Capital building, for any clues or people who didn't belong. About thirty minutes later, Officer Young handed them their licenses and a special pass that would get them through any check points along their way out of the District of Columbia.

"Mr. and Mrs. Black sorry for any inconvenience. We hope you have a good visit and come back again."

"Thank you Officer, it'll be a trip we'll never forget. Which way is the subway station?" Mr. Black asked.

"Just head up seventeenth street. You'll see the signs in a little bit."

"Thanks Officer Young. You've been a big help. I hope you catch the guy who shot at the President."

Chapter Thirty-One

At exactly twelve-thirty-five, President Watson walked into the oval Office holding a handkerchief on his ear. "Get me Governor Bent on the phone," he screamed. "Doctor, stitch this mess up as fast as you can."

"Yes sir, said the staff doctor," as he cleaned to wound.

"Mr. President, Governor Bent on line one."

"Thanks. Governor, what have you decided to do? I need you to rescind your demand for secession right now."

"I am sorry President Watson, but that's not going to happen. We are seceding and will not give in to you and the new U.S. Government."

"I can't believe you would allow innocent blood to be spilled," yelled Watson jumping up from his chair and causing the Doctor to inflict pain.

"Ouch, watch it."

"Mr. President you need to sit still so I can get this sewn up."

"Forget about it we'll do that later," he said as he waved the doctor off. "Listen Bent, you're being a blanking . . .hole! Who do you think you are! You can't win and I'll never let you get away with this. Your assassination attempt on me did nothing but make me madder. Texas will end up a pile of rubble when we get done with you."

"I don't have any idea about an assassination attempt but rest assured Mr. President, we will remember the Alamo. We will fight and we will win. Texans will die for their independence and for what's right. We've got passion behind us, something your men will never have. I would like you to stand down and let's resolve this peaceably."

"Governor, you've got just under twenty minutes to change your mind before we cross into Texas. Call me if you have a change of heart," he said slamming down the phone. "Get me the Secretary of Defense in here."

"He's waiting in the front office, sir," said the presidential aid pushing the intercom. "Send General Bennett in."

"Mr. President, I hope it's good news."

"Sorry, General, but the war is gonna take

place. Make sure your men and machinery are all in place. It's a go in eighteen minutes."

"Yes sir. I'll go inform Colonel Shields. We're all set up down in the war room. If you would like to join us, you'll be able to see every thing that takes place on the front."

"I'll be down about twelve fifty-five."

"Yes sir."

* * * * *

"Delores, please get me Colonel Bowie on the phone."

"Right away sir."

"Hello President Bent, I hope this is good news."

"I'm afraid not James. They're planning on attacking at one.. Are you ready for it?"

"We're as ready as we can be. We outnumber the ground troops but they have much better weaponry than us. We have a surprise or two up our sleeve, so I think we can stay them off for the first couple of waves. I'm hoping to get them second guessing their tactics."

"How about air cover? Do you have enough?"

"Well Mr. President, we have what we have.

So we'll make do."

"Did your man ever make it to Texas?"

"Yes, Sergeant Major Lazier along with two former Special Forces guys and a computer expert came in early this morning. The Sergeant Major has already inspected the front lines and has tweaked them and added a surprise or two for the Marines."

"What's the computer guy good for?"

"Mr. President, this kid's a genius, you need him in your office when we win this war. He's already hacked into the enemy's computer system. I can see their entire battle plan and are they in for a shock. He's been able to hijack their communications signal and we hear every order as it's given. He has almost guaranteed victory."

"I can hear the excitement in your voice Colonel. You have eighteen minutes left. I'll leave you to your command. Rest assured, we will be praying for you all."

"Thank you, Mr. president."

* * * * *

Once situated in the War Room below the Oval Office, General Randall Bennett, assessed the TV screens and gave Colonel Shields a call.

"Colonel, General Bennett here."

"Yes sir, General. Are we a go or can I hold off?"

"Unfortunately, it looks like it's a go. Are your men ready?"

"There's a lot of grumbling in the ranks, sir. They don't like the idea of a civil war especially now that they know their former Sergeant Major is on the other side."

"How'd they find that out?"

"Lazier came over to the road block and talked with my Sergeant Major, making himself known to all the Marines around. He's looked on as bigger than life in the impressionable minds of my young Marines."

"Well he's just another traitor as far as we're concerned. Make sure your men know that. Have you had any desert?"

"Yeah, a few of the Texans disappeared in the middle of Wednesday night and it looks like we lost a few more last night. I moved most of the Texans to the back units so they wouldn't have to fight their kinfolk."

"Okay Colonel, we've got the screens set for viewing on this end, the President's gonna join us for the initial wave. Good luck."

"Thank you General. Even though we have high tech weapons, it's gonna be a tough battle.

221

These Texans know how to fight and they're not afraid of us or dying. You know, as well as I do, that gives them the upper hand."

"I understand that, Colonel. I also know we have to attack them making us the easier targets. Use your missiles and air support to give you the cover you will need to get the job done."

"They've been showing us their air support all morning with fly overs. It looks like they've got some pretty decent planes and pilots on their side. We may see a dog fight in the air above us."

"Colonel, we'll try to stay in touch as you and your men move forward."

"Thank you General, I'll talk with you after it's over, sir."

Chapter Thirty-Two

James Bowie, his elbows on his desk with
his head resting in his cupped hands, began to speak
out load.

"My gracious heavenly Father,
Thank you for Your Son, Jesus Christ,
Who left heaven's glory to take on the
likeness of man. Your love for the
world is so wonderful and
magnificent."

Father, I pray that you will
intervene and stop the upcoming
battle. It is less than fifteen minutes
away and many young men will suffer
and die if they attack us. Father, it's
much more important that they have an
opportunity to know Jesus than
anything else. Lord, I know you can
put an end to this with the snap of
Your fingers and I seek that above all
else at this point. Yet, Lord, I desire

Your will above mine just as Your Son
came to do Your will.

"Father, give me the wisdom
needed as I lead my men into battle.
Your Word tells me to ask and You
will give it. Lord, I am asking for it
now. Please give me clear direction as
we fight for the freedom of Texas and
the ability to worship You, unhindered
from a godless government."

Father, bless, as only You can,
as we prepare for battle. In Jesus
name. Amen."

"Sergeant Dear," Colonel Bowie said over
the intercom.

"Yes sir."

"Have the Sergeant Major come in."

"Yes sir."

"Sergeant Major Lazier, reporting as ordered
sir."

"At ease Robert. Have a seat. You're looking
awful snazzy in that new Texas uniform."

"I think I'd rather have my blue jeans back.
These are a little bulky," he said looking down at
his pants. "Are we heading out to the front lines,
sir."

"In a couple of minutes. I thought we'd say
hi to our wives first," he said as he put his cell on

speaker phone.

"Honey, what's going on? Don't you have a war to win?" Malinda asked.

"Hey baby, Sergeant Major Lazier and I are just getting ready to head to the front and I thought we should tell our wives we love them. Is Sally right there?"

"Yes, are we on speaker?"

"Yes ma'am."

"Robert, I love you," cried Sally.

"I love you too Baby," he said leaning up to the desk where the phone was sitting. "Keep your focus on the Lord as we head out and be praying for us."

"You know we will. You keep your head down. I want to see you again on this side of heaven."

"That's my plan, Sally."

"James, we'll be praying for God's wisdom as you lead the charge," Malinda said with boldness.

"Thanks Mal, I'll need it and He'll give it. I just hope I can listen when He does."

"I'm not worried about that. You've always been able to understand God's authority in your life and I don't see any reason you would stop now. I love you, James. Be careful."

"Okay girls, we've got to head out. I'll call when it's all over," James said standing up. "Hey, before I forget, don't pay any attention to the news. It'll most likely be biased and you don't really need to see what's happening on the front lines."

"Yes sir, Colonel," Malinda said jokingly. "Call as soon as you can. We love you both."

"The feeling is mutual, honey. You gals keep your focus on the Lord. Bye."

"Let's go Sergeant Major, we don't want to be late for the party."

* * * * *

Colonel Ryan Shields, walked over to his desk, unlocked the lower bottom drawer and drew out a half empty fifth of vodka. Plopping into his chair, he unscrewed the cap and stared into the bottle for a split second before hoisting it to his lips. After two big swallows, he paused as the hot liquid burned his throat. Then two more before he locked the now quarter bottle back into the drawer, grabbed his briefcase and headed out the door.

"Colonel Shields, sir," Sergeant Major Klink said as he stood to attention.

"At ease, Sergeant Major. Give me a run down."

"Sir, we've got a lot of unrest in the rank and file. They're not liking the idea of fighting on home soil. Especially against Lazier and Bowie."

"I figured we'd have some problems. Are they gonna fight?"

"They're Marines sir, they'll fight because we tell em to fight. The problem is gonna be fighting with passion. The Texans have got all of that, we're just gonna be going through the motions and that scares me."

"Well then, Sergeant Major, let's go and instill some passion," he said stumbling as he turned.

"Sir, you okay," Klink said reaching out to keep him on his feet.

"I'm fine," he said rudely pulling his arm free.

"Sir, yes sir. We have some problems with our air support, sir," he said as he opened the door for the Colonel.

"What kind of problem? Those Pog (person other than a grunt) air jockey's got issues?" Slurred Shields.

"Apparently about half of our planes are grounded because the pilots have the flu."

"What," cried Shields. "There's no such thing as flu when we're at war. Tell em to get their butts in the cockpits."

"I talked with Lieutenant Colonel Douglas about fifteen minutes ago and he said his guys are throwing up all over the place. You can't fly a Harrier puking in your oxygen mask."

"What about getting some drones up."

"When the military downsizing took place they turned the control of all the drones to the Air Force. We didn't think we would need any for this little skirmish so we didn't ask them. It'll take half a day to get them here."

"So you're telling me we have half our air support puking their guts out and our Marines really don't want to fight," Colonel Shields screamed. "Come on, Sergeant Major, it's your mission to keep our men ready and willing to kill. We're Marines!"

"Sir, yes sir."

"Get me the company commanders on the phone."

"One at a time, sir, or as a conference call?"

"All at once. We've only got twelve minutes."

Sir, yes sir. We'll have it set in the back seat of the Humvee," snapping his fingers to the staff sergeant tagging behind them.

Climbing in the Humvee the staff sergeant handed the phone to his superior and said, "Just push this button sir and you'll be on speaker phone with your commanders."

"Thank you, sergeant. At least someone

228

knows their job," he said as he raised the corner of his mouth and raised his nose at Klink.

"Sir, I'm sorry, sir," Klink said turning his head and raising his eyes."

"Men, we are less than twelve minutes out of putting a hurt on the Texas Militia. Pump your men up and make sure they're ready to fight for the United States of America. Keep your communication lines open and be ready to go when I give the order to attack. The heavy artillery will bombard the enemy lines as your men rush in."

"Sir, what kind of air support will we have? They've been letting us know they've got plenty of planes. I assume our guys are ready to fly."

"Unfortunately, Captain, it looks like some of our boys are out with the flu. We'll only be half strength at best."

"Sir, we're Marines we can take these Texas cowboys with or without air support," The Captain said with a tentative voice.

"Captain, I hope you give the commands to your men bolder than that."

"Sir, yes sir."

"Okay I'll give the order as soon as I get it from the Commander-in-Chief."

"Sergeant Major, I'm gonna run to the head. When you see me come out of that door get me General Bennett on the phone," he said getting out of the Humvee with his briefcase.

"Yes sir."

Once in side the porta-jon, Colonel Shields

pulled out a chrome flask and took a hard and long drink. *Come on Ryan. Get a hold of yourself. You don't need this vodka. Get a grip and go out there and win this war.* The battle raged in his mind. *It's impossible to win they have you outnumbered. Your men are not wanting to fight. You have no air support. Colonel you can't possibly win. Take another nip it'll calm your nerves.* Raising the flask he finished it off and threw it down the hole.

"Here he comes, Staff Sergeant, make the call." Sergeant Major Klink said.

"You got the General for me?" Commanded Shields.

"Yes sir," handing him the phone the Staff Sergeant got out of the Humvee.

"General Bennett, we've got some problems on this end."

Chapter Thirty-Three

"What'd ya mean we got problems? We're the United States of America, they're just one Lone Star State," Secretary of Defense, General Randall Bennett said.

"The men are jittery and don't want to fight on U.S. Soil and our air support is not up to par. The pilots have some sort of flu bug."

"Colonel, we've only got six minutes before the warning is up. We need to go in and take over Texas," he said with scowl.

"I know the time and we'll attack if we have to. I'm just afraid we might get turned back and that'll give those Texans more confidence than we went them to have. Can we get a postponement until we can get more fire power out here?"

"The President's not gonna want to do that."

"Do what, General?" The President asked as he entered the war room.

"Sir, Colonel Shields would like to buy some more time before the attack."

"Colonel Shields, can you hear me?"

"Yes sir, Mr. President."

"You got five minutes and I expect you to squash this revolt. I'm not planning on giving a reprieve to these traitors," he said as he took the seat in front of the big screen. "Why would you want more time? Can't your Marines handle a few militia misfits?"

"Sir, unfortunately, half of our pilots are throwing up with the flu bug and the men don't really want to fight against their own countrymen. Their hearts are not in it. I think we would be better off until we could get some drones out here and pick off their headquarters and leaders knocking them down a peg or two."

"Are you saying we could lose this battle?" The President asked leaning forward on the arms of the chair.

"That's a real possibility sir. And if we lose this initial battle things will most likely get out of hand and other States might think they can do the same."

"Stay on the line Colonel, let me give it a minute or two."

* * * * *

On the other side of the Texas border Sergeant Major Lazier gave the orders to raise the fifty by 8 foot banners all along the front lines. Written in big bold letters were the words

REMEMBER THE ALAMO. As the banners were raised the entire Texas Militia yelled the same words. "Remember the Alamo, and then let out a load Texas "Ye-ha," as they quietly ran down into the front line trenches and positioned themselves for battle.

Five hundred yards across the border six hundred young Marines, eyes wide, looked at each other in disbelief. The rumbling in the ranks of the U.S. Marines grew to a small roar.

"Colonel Shields. Did you hear that," exclaimed Sergeant Major Klink.

"Man, I sure did. We need to stop this attack. We don't have a chance at this point."

"Only two minutes left sir."

"Mr. President, sir. I need an answer now." Shields said boldly. "We cannot win this first battle with what we have in place. They are gonna kick our butts, sir. I've got Colonel Bowie on the other line. What do you want me to tell him."

"Colonel Shields, tell him that in two minutes we are gonna attack, unless he backs down," he said angrily. "If he doesn't back down then give him forty-eight more hours."

"Yes sir."

"Colonel Bowie, I beg of you to stand down now, before we both lose a number of good men.

Please James, I don't want to fight you."

"I can't do that, Ryan. My orders are to hold my position and you know I'll do that until my dying breath."

"In that case I've been given orders to wait another forty-eight hours. President Watson wants to try to do this peaceably. He's given a reprieve but it will be the last one."

"Thank you, Lord!"

"Don't thank Him. I'm the one who argued for an extension," Shields slurred. "You know I don't believe in your God, James."

"Ryan, maybe someday, we can talk again about why I believe in Him. I know the only reason you stopped this is because you couldn't win. I suppose we'll meet on another day."

"We will, James, and you will lose your bid for secession. Same place in forty-eight hours. In case you didn't figure it out, your precious Sunday will be a bloody day for Texas."

Other fiction work by Dennis Snyder available through Amazon:

Personal Vengeance: Lake Haven Murders series book one

The golf Course Massacre: Lake Haven Murders series book two

Road Rage vs. Forgiveness --- A short story

Non-Fiction work by Dennis Snyder available for Kindle or Nook

Proof of Heaven: From the Bible not Near Death Experiences

Angelology: The Study of Angels, Good and Bad

The Seven Deadly Sins (Coming February 28)

The above titles are from the "Looking at Life Through the Grid of the Bible Series"

The Importance of Prayer